What the reviewers are saying about

Private PROPERTY

…a refreshingly touching twist to the ménage theme

~ The Romance Studio

Leah Braemel's PRIVATE PROPERTY delves into all of
one woman's naughty fantasies and promises to leave
readers hot and sweaty

~ Romance Junkies

…a spicy erotic novella

~ Joyfully Reviewed

Private PROPERTY

LEAH BRAEMEL

Somerlane
Publishing

For information contact:

Leah Braemel **http://leahbraemel.com**

Cover Design by Flirtation Designs

ISBN-13: 978-0-9879304-9-1

First Edition: August 2016

10 9 8 7 6 5 4 3 2 1

Author's Note

When I first wrote PRIVATE PROPERTY, Jodi Tyler and Mark Rodriguez had already been dating for a while. So when I was invited by my then-editor at Samhain Publishing to write a short holiday-themed story for their newsletter, I figured FIRST NIGHT was a perfect way to introduce Jodi and Mark and talk about how their no-strings affair had started.

In 2012, with self publishing becoming easier and more acceptable, I expanded the story, introduced some of reasons Mark is selling his company to Sam, as well as giving a bit more depth to Jodi and Mark, then published FIRST NIGHT so everyone could read it again.

Now self-publishing has given me the option of offering it to you as a bonus read with this new print version of PRIVATE PROPERTY.

Enjoy!

Leah Braemel

First NIGHT

When it comes to her love life, security specialist Jodi Tyler has hit a dry spell the size of the Sahara. Not to mention her track record for choosing guys who aren't threatened by a strong woman isn't the best. When a friend at the company's New Year's Eve party issues a challenge to seduce their boss, the uber sexy Mark Rodriguez, Jodi accepts.

The last thing Mark Rodriguez needs right now is another distraction. His company is under attack and he's desperately trying to hold it together. When the blonde bombshell he hired as his second-in-command struts into the room and straddles his lap, who is he to turn her down? Especially with her offer of a no-strings-attached affair.

But when the clock strikes midnight, and the ball drops on Times Square, has Jodi won the bet or lost her heart?

CHAPTER ONE

It might have been the two glasses of champagne that drove Jodi Tyler to consider her friend Terri's dare. Or maybe, she told herself for the fifth time, she really was concerned her boss was working himself too hard.

Over Hector's attempts at singing and the amps blasting full-power, Jodi could barely hear a word of Terri's explanation. The music itself wasn't bad—Juan and Tyrell both played a mean guitar—but Hector needed to be muzzled for mangling U2's *New Year's Day* so badly.

Champagne sloshing over the side of her wine glass, Terri gestured toward their boss, who stood in the farthest corner, his cell phone pressed to one ear and a hand covering the other. The suit jacket Mark Rodriguez had worn earlier was nowhere in sight. His tie had disappeared too, leaving the top two buttons of his shirt splayed open. What was it about that peek-a-boo V that she found so attractive? He twisted to allow a waiter to pass, which caused his shirt sleeve to pull taut. Damn, the man must work out five hours a day to maintain those shoulder muscles.

Though he had an excellent physique his recently-earned MBA spoke to his intelligence, a trait Jodi found just as sexy as his kick-ass body.

From the deep furrow in his forehead, whoever he was talking to was pissing him off. Bingo, there was his tell of running his hand over his head, something he only did when he was trying to keep his cool. Normally he kept his dark hair trimmed in a Marine's high and tight, but he'd been so harried lately, he'd let the top part grow longer. Long enough that every time she'd seen him, she'd been tempted to run her fingers through it.

Poor guy. Celada Security had the best rep in the Metroplex, yet the damned competition kept swiping clients by undercutting their rates. It wasn't that Mark was doing anything wrong—the man had a flair for keeping both his clients and his employees happy—but he didn't have the type of money their competition did. Which meant this might be the last party they'd all celebrate together. Unless he pulled off whatever Hail Mary pass he'd hinted at during today's staff meeting.

Terri put her mouth to Jodi's ear and repeated, "Come on, Jodi. Mark brought his laptop to the party, and when he's not working on it, he's been on that damned phone. You need to get him to loosen up."

Jodi rolled her eyes. "And just how do you propose I do that?"

Terri flattened her free hand over her stomach and wiggled her hips. "There's no better way to start a New Year than with some hot monkey sex."

"Terri!" Laughing at her friend's antics, Jodi shoved Terri's shoulder.

"Jodi." Terri mimicked Jodi's exasperation. "He's not seeing anyone, and neither are you since you finally saw the light about Jace and kicked him to the curb. Sex is the perfect way to relax and, honey, you both need to relax. Besides, I've seen the way you eye Mark when you think no one's looking. You're dying to get him naked."

"I am not!" Yes, I am. I want to pull his shirt off and run my fingers—hell my tongue—down his pecs, over his abs. To trace that line of dark hair from his navel to where it hides beneath his fly.

"It's time you get back up on the horse and Mark's the perfect stallion to ride." Terri grabbed a champagne flute from a passing waiter and pressed it into Jodi's hand. "Here. Give him this. Tell him there's a private party and he's invited. I bet he'll have you seeing fireworks before the ball drops in Times Square."

As Jodi argued internally about whether it was a good idea to have sex with the boss—which she knew wasn't smart at the best of times—Terri fumbled in her purse, withdrew a package and shoved it in Jodi's bag. Jodi peered inside to see what her friend had given her. "Holy crap, you brought a box of condoms to the party? What the fuck were you expecting? An orgy?"

"No. But it never hurts for a girl to be prepared."

With an entire box? Terri obviously had far more to her beneath that standard Celada uniform than she let on.

"You know you've been fantasizing about him for months. It's time you go hook up with him and ride that man into the sunset." Terri shoved her in Mark's direction. "Or let him ride you."

What the heck am I doing? Jodi asked herself, as she

maneuvered her way through the crowded room.

Taking responsibility for your own happiness, that's what.

Wouldn't it be great to have a partner take charge in the bedroom? How many meetings with Mark had she left totally turned on? How she knew he'd be the type of guy she needed, she couldn't say exactly, but she sensed some carefully controlled wildness that matched her needs. And then there was his latent sensuality.

So she'd invite him up to her room, see if the fantasy matched reality. If it didn't, it would be a one and done, the itch scratched, and they'd move on.

When Mark edged out of the room, she switched directions and followed him into the hall. Except he was nowhere in sight.

"Damn it, where'd he go? He was here a minute ago."

She called to a nearby Celada Security employee, who was chatting up one of the tuxedo-clad waitresses. "Hey, Cody? Did you see where Mark went?"

Without taking his eyes off the waitress, Cody used his chin to point down the hall. "Try the Hospitality Suite."

Mark had left the door partially open, so she slipped

in without knocking and closed the door behind her. She hesitated for a second then threw the deadbolt. Decision made, she faced what could destroy her career.

Damn, it wasn't just a sitting room with only the desk, a couch and a couple of chairs. It was a freaking suite in the full sense of the word, complete with a king-size bed in the room beyond. There went that long-held fantasy of a guy taking her standing up against the wall.

Mark sat at the typical table that hotels laughingly called a desk, concentrating on the laptop open in front of him. "Yeah, I know, Sam, but Martin's got me by the short hairs. He's underbid me on the Huffman Oil contract and, from the sounds of it, he's going after the Gottfried account as well. I sure could use some advice." Given the tiny green light of the webcam, Mark was in a video chat, but from where she was standing, she couldn't see the image on the screen.

"I'm real sorry, buddy, but you don't have the pockets needed to go up against that asshole long-term." Even though the guy's voice was liquid sex, she still preferred Mark's Latino-tinged accent. "Sure, he's running through his inheritance like it's water, but we both know he'll last longer than the banks'll give you. Take my offer—it's the only way your company will survive."

Offer? This Sam could help Mark keep Celada? Hell yeah, take the loan and flip the bird to the competition.

"I appreciate it but I'll need some time to think about it, okay?"

"I hear you, but don't leave it too long. You remember what happened back in college? When you waited to ask out that smokin' hot babe in Professor Brennan's third year justice class?"

"Sharon, yeah, I remember her." Mark's rumbling laughter had Jodi clenching her thighs together at the sudden ache that developed. Why did the one guy who got her hot have to be her boss? Why couldn't he just be some guy she'd met at the party? "I also remember she ended up in your bed."

"Hey, she approached me, remember? You had your chance, and you blew it."

"More like she blew you."

"She wasn't your type, and you know it." Sam's voice changed, as if he was worried Mark still bore a grudge, though from what Jodi could tell, Mark was more amused than annoyed. "Look, I was serious about my offer."

"I know."

"I've been playing with the numbers this morning. Maybe it'll help you make up your mind. I can either give you a cash payout or you can take ten percent out in stock. And you get to keep running things in the Dallas office, and any other offices we decide to open in Texas."

Shit. Not a loan, a buyout.

"I'll think about it." The ruckus in the hallway grew louder. "Look, Sam, there's a party filled with my people I need to get back to and, from the looks of that tux, you're at one, too."

"They won't miss me for a while. Listen, Mark. I'm not going to pressure you—sounds like you've got enough without me addin' to it. What you need to do is hook up with that fine lookin' blonde you said you had your eye on. You know what they say about sex bein' a great stress reliever."

Was she the blonde? Or did she have competition? Jodi's jaw clenched at the thought that Mark might turn to someone else. Jeez Louise, Tyler, get a grip. Here you are talking about having a one-and-done with him and yet you're jealous that he might want to sleep with someone else?

"What did you say about her last week?" Sam continued. "*Ese cuerpo con tanta curvas y yo sin frenos?*"

Damn it, she really needed to enroll in some Spanish classes. Especially since they spoke for at least five minutes before Sam switched back to English. "Go find that girl and get nekkid and sweaty."

Sheesh, did Terri get to this Sam guy as well? What was with everyone lately?

"Hey, you know what?" Sam continued. "I could fly out there and deliver the contracts to you and we can double up the way we used to back in the day. I wouldn't mind blowin' off some steam."

"Not with one of my employees, you don't."

Holy crap, it was her they were talking about. There were no other blondes working at Celada. Unless you counted Jason, Steve or Seb. Which she didn't.

Sam's soft laughter floated across the room. "Like that is it? Feelin' a little protective of her? Territorial? Or are you afraid I'm going to steal her away from you? Because I won't, buddy. I give you my word."

"If you met her, you'd be offering her a job that she couldn't refuse and, next thing I know, I lose my best operative as well as my company."

"She's that good, huh?"

"Better than good. Jodi's…an amazing operative,

Sam." Mark rubbed the back of his neck, another sign she recognized that meant he was feeling stressed, though this time she wondered if it was about Martin or if Sam had struck some nerve. "If you do come out here, she's hands-off, d'you hear?"

"If she's as good as you say," Sam's tone turned serious, "you'd better make sure you keep her happy or Martin'll snatch her away from you. He'd do it just to twist your tail, and he can afford to pay her whatever she asks."

Like hell she'd go to work for that snake-in-the-grass.

"Look, I've gotta go. I'll get back to you about your offer—whether I take it or not, thanks. And thanks for offering to leave me in charge—given the mess things are right now, I appreciate the vote of confidence."

"I wouldn't offer it if I didn't trust you, Mark. You're up against an asshole with deep pockets and no conscience—I've got your back."

"Thanks, Sam. Oh, and Happy New Year." The call ended, then Mark cursed softly as he tapped something into the keyboard.

Was she really going to do this?

Determined, she set her purse on the floor and

stepped farther into the room. "Are you going to take his offer?"

Mark looked around in surprise. "How long have you been listening?"

"Probably too long for your comfort," she admitted. She perched on the edge of the desk and held out the flute of champagne. "You look like you need this."

"Thanks." He took the glass and leaned back in his chair, contemplating the bubbling liquid before taking a sip.

Up close the dark circles ringing Mark's gorgeous brown eyes seemed even deeper. Shoot, even if she had a horrible propensity for animal metaphors, Terri was right; Mark was running himself into the ground. "I didn't mean to eavesdrop but who's Sam?"

"Sam is Sam Watson—he owns Hauberk Protection."

Jodi managed to keep her jaw from dropping. She would have had to been blind and deaf to not have heard the story of how Sam Watson had bought a small going-nowhere firm and turned it into one of the biggest private protection firms on the East Coast over the past five years.

So he was looking to expand west now, was he? It

could be a huge opportunity. A win-win for everyone. Except Mark, who had once told her he'd always dreamed of owning his own company.

"Do you trust him? I mean, it's one thing to say he'll leave you in charge, but once he has ownership…"

He nodded. "Yeah. I trust him. Besides, I wouldn't sign Celada over to him without getting everything in writing. And one of my top concerns is my employees, so I'll make sure he guarantees to keep everyone on for at least two years. From what I've researched, the Hauberk people get better benefits, better pensions. Things I've not been able to afford to offer."

"But if it weren't for this hostile take-over thing, you wouldn't consider selling Celada, would you?"

Mark pursed his lips. "You know, if Sam had come to me with his offer a year ago, even then I'd have been insane to turn it down."

"It's that good?"

"Better than I could have asked from anyone else. Since he runs in some pretty high circles in DC, we can bring in even more clients just using the Hauberk banner."

"But you're not sure."

"No. I know it's the logical thing to do. It's a good

business decision. Sam's said I'd have stock, and earlier he said he'd put me in charge of western operations."

"But you need to step back. Think about it with a clear head." She held out her hand. "Why don't you come back to the party? Sam was right—you need to blow off some steam."

Mark sighed and finished off the last of the champagne before gesturing to his laptop. "As much as I'm tempted, I can't afford to slack off tonight. I've got to get the Gottfried bid in line."

"I'm not saying," she said softly, as she took his champagne glass from him and set it on the desk, "that you stop work entirely. I'm just suggesting you take a short break. A couple of hours, that's all."

He shook his head. "As tempting as that sounds, I can't."

"Going to be stubborn, huh?" Before he could stop her, she snapped the lid of the laptop closed. "Office is closed for the day, boss." After nudging his chair with her knee until his back faced her, she started massaging his shoulders. Holy cow, the man had muscles to rival an Olympic swimmer and they were tied up in knots.

"Hey! What do you think you're doing?"

"Helping you relax."

"Jodi, as much as I appreciate it, I'm your boss, and this isn't appropriate." Yet he wasn't pulling away.

She leaned down and whispered in his ear. "Remember, I heard you and Sam talking, and even though I don't speak Spanish, I know you're interested in me. Well, guess what? The feeling is mutual."

CHAPTER TWO

This wasn't happening. He'd fallen asleep in the chair and was dreaming. That could be the only logical explanation. Because the kick-ass, business-like Jodi Tyler he'd hired wouldn't be giving him a massage and suggesting they have sex. Interested in him was a metaphor for wanting to have sex with him, wasn't it? She'd always been a straight talker, so why was she talking in metaphors now? Please God, let her be talking in metaphors.

She released his shoulders and spun his chair around. Leaning over him, she placed her hands on the arms of the chair, trapping him in place. "And before you start thinking I'm only doing this because I'm expecting a promotion or special treatment from you, I'm not. I'm just trying to help you relax."

If she had been any other woman, he'd have taken up her invitation without a second thought, especially tonight. *Ay carajo*, instead of the standard Celada uniform of white shirt and grey dress pants she normally wore, tonight she was one hot package. From how her hair draped over her shoulder and into her cleavage, and the sparkly, clingy number she wore that accentuated her curves, to her long legs, highlighted so spectacularly by a pair of red stilettos.

Damn, she had some mighty fine curves. What he'd give to be inside her, feeling that beautiful flesh riding his.

What are you thinking? She's your employee.

She stroked her fingers through his hair, sending electrical shocks straight to his cock. Goddamn, the woman had him as hard as stone and she'd barely touched him.

This could come back and bite you on the ass.

I'd rather bite her on the ass.

He placed his hands over his groin and muttered, "*¡Ay Dios mío!*"

"As Sam said, sex is a great stress reliever." She

leaned closer, until her mouth was next to his ear. Her voice had a Lauren Bacall huskiness that had his balls aching.

"No strings attached. We forget that you're my boss. We're just two people who hooked up at a New Year's Eve party."

He stilled beneath her fingers. There was no way to misinterpret that invitation. "Let me get this straight. You're volunteering to have sex with me. No questions asked. And you're not drunk or doing this as a bet or because you feel pressured in any way?"

A familiar 'you are such a doofus' look flickered across her face. Not that she'd ever directed it at him before, but his mother and sisters had often enough. Did all women practice it in a mirror or something?

"I'm doing this of my own free accord. I've had a single glass of champagne, so no, I'm not drunk." Her hand slid from his hair, down his neck and over the opening of his shirt, until she touched his fly. "All I'm proposing is one night of no strings attached sex."

Aw, hell. What man with a hard-on ready to erupt like Mount Vesuvius could turn down an offer like that? He gave in to temptation and stroked her hair, marveling at not only how soft it was but how it gleamed pure gold against his tanned skin.

"What do you say, Mark? Do we have a deal? You ready for a little R&R?"

The breathy hitch in her voice told him there was no misunderstanding her intention.

He caught her hand. "Are you aware of what I might ask of you?"

Her gaze dropped to the tent in his pants, then slowly raised to meet his. The heat in her eyes seared a path all the way up his chest. "I'll be at your command for the night. In the bed. Up against the wall. Or on the floor if you prefer. Whatever you say, I'll do."

He forced his mind from the image of tying her hands behind her, of pressing her to her knees, when he realized she was still talking.

She ran a finger along his jaw, tracing her thumb over his lips. "Just tell me what you want."

He pulled her toward him so she tumbled onto his lap. He cupped her head with one hand until her mouth hovered a hairsbreadth from his. "Let's start with this."

Despite the danger signals ringing in his head, he couldn't pull back if someone held a knife to his balls. She tasted of champagne, and paradise. There was no hesitation from her when he slid his tongue past the part in her lips, no regrets, no second thoughts. If anything, there was a tenderness he'd rarely experienced, and never expected from his hard-ass operative.

Everything about her softened, and when he stroked her throat she leaned into his touch. A need to protect her, to treat her gently, while at the same time the need to master her roared over him.

Jodi tugged his shirt from his pants, slipping her hands under the fabric, splaying her fingers over his abdomen.

Each press of her fingers against his flesh left trails of fire, of need, in their wake. No woman he'd been with before had affected him like this. What was it about her that made him want to handcuff her to him, to guard her from any other man's sight? Not breaking the kiss, he deftly undid the buttons of her dress until the silky fabric slithered off her breasts. Light pink nipples peeked out from beneath a white lacy concoction that he quickly undid. The moment her nipples were freed, he licked and suckled, kissed and nipped her flesh.

Her breath caught deep in her throat when he slipped his hand beneath the slit in her skirt. He caught her cries with a kiss, stopping them from going farther. He'd be damned if anyone out in the hall would hear them. A comment at the wrong time, to the wrong person could destroy her career. When he made to move away, she caught his hand. "I've locked the door. No one's going to walk in on us."

So she really had planned to make the offer. It hadn't been a spur of the moment decision.

He caressed the silk-smooth skin of her thighs then went higher. A soft breathy moan floated out of her when his fingers met bare skin. Holy crap, she'd gone commando.

He paused. Waiting. Would she change her mind? Would she stop him?

Her eyes, lids heavy, lifted and met his. Her hips rolled against his hand as her tongue darted out, licked her lips, before she breathed, "Please."

As happy as he was to indulge her, the chair wasn't comfortable. Nor did he want to take her here. He wanted her in the bed, beneath him, on top of him, lying beside him the entire night.

"Stand up."

Uncertainty filled her eyes as she hesitated.

"We're not stopping. But I need you to stand. You did say you'd obey me."

Her eyes widened and she stood, her dress dropping

over her hips to pool at her feet. He slipped an arm behind her knees and lifted her, carrying her into the bedroom. Skin so soft, her light perfume and the scent of her arousal teasing his nose. So different from the tough exterior she projected in the office.

He'd never done anything as romantic as carry a woman before, and where the idea came to him this time he'd wonder about later, but holding her in his arms mingled power with intimacy, a heady combination that had his cock hardening.

Once they were in the bedroom, he laid her on the bed. Intent on getting skin-to-skin with her again, he toed off his shoes. When she reached for his fly, he caught her hands. "No. If you touch me right now, this evening is over."

She dropped her hands and lay back on the pillows, her eyes dark, as he quickly stripped himself. With each piece of clothing he divested, her breath quickened, and her skin flushed. A simple shift of her body widened her legs, allowing him a glimpse of her glistening labia. God, she was beautiful.

Letting his trousers and shirt drop on the floor, he climbed onto the bed beside her. Her skin was softer than silk against his, as warm and inviting as the expression in her eyes.

He lost track of time as he explored her body, discovering what she liked and what she didn't. Her eyes closed and her head fell back, and she reacted with a soft pant to each touch, to each kiss. His balls ached by the time he slid one finger, then another, inside her tight passage. Her soft and sweet moan trickled into his soul, held him captivated by her sensuality.

Her whole body quivered, tightening around him. Trailing his thumb on either side of her clit, he stroked her and teased her body, inside and out, until her eyes went glassy and the first flutters of her impending orgasm tickled his fingers. He backed off, and then started all over again.

And again.

Her hair cascaded over his arm, her nipples were hard buds enticing him to taste them again. So he did. A lick and a taste, a nip and her back arched, her body clamping around his fingers as she flew apart.

So beautiful. So fucking beautiful. He slowed his strokes, easing her down, whispering how beautiful she was, thanking her for trusting him. Thanking whatever or whoever had led her into the room this night.

Her body still trembling, she raised passion-filled

eyes to his. Her hands slid from his biceps where she'd held on so tightly and down over his chest. The moment her fingers grazed his shaft, his balls drew up to his body in anticipation. He couldn't stop his gasp when she flicked her thumb over the head, spreading the bead of come welling at the tip.

Nor could he stop her when she shifted and pressed him onto his back, then nestled between his thighs. His groan started in his belly as her hair drifted over his thighs, deepened when she ran her tongue up his length. His fingers tangled in her hair, a futile attempt to hold her in check. The world around them reduced to each swirl of her tongue over the straining head.

"*Me vuelves loco.*"

CHAPTER THREE

The growled Spanish sent shivers down Jodi's back in waves. From the way his face scrunched up, and his fingers tightened in her hair, she drove him as crazy as he'd driven her. Allowing herself a private grin, Jodi vowed to make him lose his mind completely. She bent to her self-assigned task, swallowing him deep, alternately sucking and tormenting him.

His already hard shaft grew harder, silky fluid leaked from the tip onto her tongue. She moaned her own need, another orgasm fluttering in the distance despite the mind-blowing one he'd just given her. The grip on her hair tightened in a delicious lick of pain, and his hips arched up, pressing him deeper into her mouth in frantic thrusts. More warmth spilled into her mouth until he pulled her away, his voice hoarse, "*Te necesito. Un cuerpo hecho para tocar.*"

God, it made her so hot to hear him revert to Spanish. The *necesito* was obviously necessary or necessity, but the rest? "What did you say?"

"You have a body made to be touched. I want to finish inside you, baby." His eyes had darkened with passion and she shivered as a strange feeling clamped around her heart at his diminutive. She didn't want to get into a relationship; not with her history of guys walking away after shattering her heart into pieces. But she knew without a doubt that despite her promise of no strings attached, whatever was forging between them wouldn't end when the clock struck twelve.

He released her hair, hauling her up until she straddled him. "Ride me, *querida*."

Terri's metaphor about him being a stallion sprang to mind; Jodi couldn't stop herself from chuckling.

"What's so funny?"

Unwilling to break the mood, she shook her head. She positioned herself over his entrance, then stopped. Damn it, she'd left her purse—and its precious cargo— out in the other room. "Have you got a condom?"

"Damn it, how did I forget that?" He twisted beneath her, seeking the trousers he'd discarded on the floor. He withdrew a gold foil packet. She plucked it from his fingers and ripped it open, then took her time smoothing it over his length. Sweat beaded on his forehead and her own body begged to be filled by the time she finished.

Placing her hands on his shoulders, she shifted until her pussy hovered just above his shaft. "By the way," she said with a grin. "You can't come until the stroke of midnight. Think you can last that long, stud?"

Heat flared in his chocolate brown eyes. "Oh, yeah. But same goes for you. You can't come before me—we come together."

Which meant she'd delay this as long as she could. After a nod of agreement, she lowered herself slowly over his shaft, drawing simultaneous gasps from them both. Oh crap, she may have misjudged how long she could hold out. He filled her so completely, and that curve made his head hit just the right spots. Oh God, she wanted to come. Right frickin' now! But she'd be damned if she'd come before him.

All plans to slowly torture him were forgotten with the first slow glide back. He'd primed her body so well, each slide of his shaft against her inner walls had her shuddering.

He covered her face in tiny kisses, murmuring in Spanish, each tender phrase causing all coherent thought to vanish in a fiery blaze. She realized she'd lost all control when he grasped her hips and thrust deeper.

"You feel so good inside me," she moaned. There was no way in hell she was going to hold off her orgasm until midnight.

"No, you don't." He banded his arms around her and, before she knew it, she was flat on her back, staring up at him. "Wrap your legs around my waist."

Without thought, she obeyed. The new angle tilted her hips until the head of his cock hit that special spot again. Her legs shook with need.

"Put your hands above your head. Hang on to the headboard."

But that meant she wouldn't be able to touch him. To dig her fingers into his ass.

"Now, *querida*."

Oh fuck, his growled command had her body clenching around his cock, her orgasm hovering seconds away. In every relationship before this, she'd always been the one in charge, yet here she was, happy to oblige him by doing whatever he wanted. Satisfaction flared in his eyes when she lifted her arms the way he'd demanded.

He bent his head to her breasts, teasing her flesh with his tongue and his teeth. If nothing else, the man had quickly learned the way around her body and, unlike many of her previous lovers, was intent on making sure she got as much pleasure out of the night as he did.

As much as she might never be able to stand in his office or have him walk past her without her remembering him like this, Jodi already knew she would never look back on the night with regret.

DAMN, HOW COULD THERE NOT BE STEAM COMING OFF THEM BOTH? Mark thrust deep inside her, unable to maintain his normally rigid control. He'd never had such problems controlling his climax, but something about her drove him crazy.

Her head tilted back, exposing her graceful neck. Her gasp and a different, guttural sound, combined with the flutters of her impending orgasm, slammed him.

Yeah, that's the spot she liked. He buried himself again, ensuring the head of his cock stroked her hard in the same place.

Her thighs tightened about him, pulling him deeper than he thought possible. Her inner muscles quivered and rippled, caressing him. The look on her face, of bliss, of passion, entranced him. His balls tight against his body, he pulled out until only the head of his cock remained within her.

If he plunged back into her now, there was no way he'd be able to hold back. As stupid as it would sound if he said it aloud, her challenge about not coming before midnight was a challenge he wanted to win.

If this was going to be a one-time shot, he wanted it to be good for her. Needed it to be the best fucking sex she'd ever had. And not because of his own ego. There was something about her that made him want to do right by her. Be his best for her.

Letting go of one hip, he moved his hand to her core, then flicked his thumb over her clit.

Shit, that was a big mistake. Even though only part of him was inside, she clamped around his overly sensitive head, her entire body shaking in her attempt to delay her orgasm.

He dipped his head, placed his mouth near her ear. Dear God, her scent, something floral and fresh, would make him hard if she wore it around him after this. "Stop fighting it. Let yourself feel me inside you, how I fill you."

"Oh fuck!" She arched beneath him, pressing her breasts into his chest. "Stop talking and just fuck me."

His pleasure. With a growl, he plunged deep, withdrew and pounded into her. His world reduced to the sound of flesh slapping on flesh, of her pants and his, and the beautiful woman beneath him as she dug both heels into his ass. When his teeth closed about one nipple, she tipped over the edge.

Mark drew his head back, and shouted hoarsely, holding himself still as her body clutched at his shaft. It didn't help him stay in control. Lights exploded in the back of his eyes, the familiar sensation pulsed from his lower back, through his balls.

Mark caught his breath and realized he was crushing Jodi. He rolled to the side with a "be right back." After a quick trip to the bathroom to dispose of the condom and clean up, he returned to the scent of sex filling the room and strains of Auld Lang Syne being mangled both in the hallway and the courtyard outside.

When they'd arrived at the party, both without a date, he'd hoped he'd be close to her so he could wrangle his way to giving her a New Year's kiss when the ball dropped. Huh, instead he'd fucked her until his balls emptied. Happy New Year indeed.

He paused at the side of the bed, his cock semi-hard simply from the sight of Jodi lying sprawled face down on the bed, one arm buried beneath a pillow. The ass he'd told Sam was so bitable lay on full display, an open invitation to touch its warm curves, to spank it. Unable to resist, he cupped the warm flesh, his imagination filling with all sorts of games he wanted to play for the rest of the night. But for now he'd let her rest. The mattress dipped beneath him as he crawled in beside her.

With a content sigh, she cuddled against him, nestling her head in the crook of his shoulder. He pressed his lips against her hair and whispered, "Happy New Year."

Her breath was warm on his skin as she murmured an unintelligible response. She felt good there. Right. Like she belonged.

As their breathing evened out, he stroked Jodi's arms, marveling at the muscle hidden beneath her soft skin, skimmed his fingertips down her side and along the long leg curled over his hip. Her body softened against his as she drifted into sleep. Huh, normally he was the one who passed out after sex, and here she was falling asleep, while he…he was energized. Ready to take her all over again. Against the wall, her legs clamped around his waist. On her knees in front of him, her hands bound behind her. If he was lucky, she'd agree to wear a leather bustier that left her breasts free for him to play with. *Ay Dios*, he couldn't wait to see her lips closed over his cock, those beautiful blue eyes staring up at him as she sucked him off.

What was he thinking? He couldn't do this again. He shouldn't have had sex with her this time. He could have opened himself up to a potential sexual harassment lawsuit. Hell, she could even have been a plant sent by his competition, intent on blackmailing him.

Yet he trusted her. Implicitly. She would never betray him.

Why had he agreed to this being a one night deal? He had to find a way to change her mind. Something had happened tonight, some change in him or them both, that he didn't want to lose.

CHAPTER FOUR

W as there anything better after a good bout of sex than lying in a comfortable bed, the guy still awake, touching you, instead of having him grab his clothes and run out the door?

It's not that she'd ever been short of guys who wanted to date her, but most of them ran off once they discovered she was stronger than them. Her smart mouth and attitude hadn't scared Mark away. If anything it had challenged him. Tonight might have started out just about scratching an itch, but at some point something had changed between them. Some connection had been forged.

She should have known Mark would be different.

Maybe that's what had attracted her to him in the first place. Why had she accepted Terri's dare? God what a fool she was, thinking she could walk away after tonight and not remember him as the best lover she'd ever had. She shivered as fear ran with spiked boots in her chest. This couldn't turn into an all-out relationship. Relationships and her just didn't suit. Guys didn't like a strong woman with her own mind. They wanted someone who earned less than them, couldn't shoot as well. Okay, so Jace had equaled her in pay, and was an equal shot, but he'd been an asshole about her hours, and hated when she initiated sex.

"Sssh." Keeping one arm wrapped around her, Mark pulled the duvet over them both and pulled her closer, both arms closing around her as if to guard her from the external chill he thought she felt. "Go back to sleep."

The huskiness of his voice, the tenderness, sent shivers through her once again. Why did he have to be so nice? So thoughtful. Someone she'd want to see again. And again. It was going to be hell going back to being on the other side of the desk from him. To know how it felt to be held by him, to smell that delicious spicy aftershave he wore and always be reminded of their single night together.

Just keep it light. She eased back, trying to duck under his arms. Ignore how cold the cotton is compared to his body. Pretend you don't want to crawl back on top of him and feel his chest hair tickle your breasts again. To get him hard and ride him like he'd demanded at the start of the night.

His grip tightened. "If you're thinking of leaving, you promised me a whole night. That you'd do whatever I wanted."

Normally she'd be walking out the door, relieved that they were finished, happy to be returning to her own place. Why was she so happy that she might have extra time alone with him? She allowed herself to be pulled back into his embrace. Gave herself permission to trail her fingers down his chest. "So how are you feeling? Relaxed? Or do you still have some kinks that need to be worked out."

Oh crap, talk about a face/palm moment. Did she have to have worded it like that?

From the way his lips pulled apart, revealing his perfect white teeth, a startling contrast against his tanned skin, he'd caught the slip too. "Oh, baby, I have a lot of kinks I need to work out. And since we ushered out the old year in such a spectacular way, I plan to celebrate the new year with even more flair."

She just bet he had all sorts of ideas of what they could do. Count her in for every one.

Wait a minute. They'd ushered out the old year, past tense? She lifted herself until she could see the alarm clock on the far bedside table. Just as she'd suspected. "Technically it's not the new year yet. There's still fifty-four minutes left until midnight."

As if he didn't believe her, he twisted beneath her to check the clock for himself. "But they were singing Auld Lang Syne earlier…"

"That was the ball dropping in New York."

He fell back against the pillows with the most devil-ish gleam in his eyes, one that had her body both tensing and heating at what he might have planned. The smile was quickly replaced by a frown. One that worried her. "I didn't plan on having sex tonight so I only had the one condom. I may have to make a run downstairs for more."

THANK GOD FOR TERRI. Because if Mark left, he might decide not to return. Now she'd had a sample of a night with him, she wasn't prepared to give it up so soon. "As it happens, I have some extras."

Mark's eyebrows arched. "Extras. Plural? Just what were you planning for tonight?"

"I didn't plan to approach you tonight. It just sort of happened."

"Any regrets?"

She searched deep inside. Worries that this could go sour, plenty. Regrets? She shook her head. "None. You?"

There was no hesitation. "None."

"Then I guess we'd better get you suited up." She hopped off the bed. Aware of his gaze locked on her ass, she sauntered into the front room and retrieved the condoms.

His grin lightened his face again when she returned. From the way his cock was standing at attention already, they might end up using a good portion of the box before the end of the night.

He took the box she held out. "You realize I could have ordered them through room service?"

She stifled a snort as she imagined the conversation between him and the desk clerk as he placed the order. *What type would you like, sir? Ribbed, extra-large, please.* "Just open the box!"

While he fought the plastic covering, she allowed

herself to fully appreciate his body, from the muscled shoulders and pecs, to the dark nest of hair at the base of his cock.

Would he bind her and blindfold her? She could definitely get into that type of action. Although being bound with her hands behind her back might limit her riding him the way he'd originally demanded. And it ruled out up-against-the-wall sex.

Once he'd opened the box, she plucked one of the packets and kept her voice casual. "Let's make the night interesting."

"You think I'm going to bore you?"

"Not at all, but I'm thinking of a wager. Whoever can last longest before having an orgasm has to…" What should she demand?

"Has to serve the other breakfast in bed for the next four Saturdays. Sundays too."

The speed at which Mark supplied a reward surprised her. As did what he demanded. Until she saw the intensity of his gaze. He cupped her jaw, his touch gentle but firm. "If I can make you come first, we continue this. Tomorrow. The next day. We try dating. We see where this thing we have between us goes."

Her breath stuttered in her chest. "I don't know if that's a good idea."

"I know. I'm your boss and it makes things awkward. But there's something between us that I can't deny. Haven't you felt it too?"

"I don't do relationships well, Mark. I screw them up."

His lips firmed as if he didn't believe her. "Then let's not call it a relationship. Just say we're friends with benefits."

Fuck buddies. She could do that. "Okay, but with no strings attached."

"There will be one string. I'll be the only *friend* who has that particular type of *benefit*. If I discover you've slept with anyone else, everything resets."

Despite how it sounded exactly the same as a relationship, she nodded. "Same goes for you."

She pulled him back to her and kissed him lightly on the lips. *It's just an affair. No emotions involved.* God, he smelled so great, and tasted even better. *Yeah, you keep telling yourself that.* Trailing her fingers down his back until she cupped his ass, she murmured, "You think you can last another hour, stud?"

His lips smiled against hers and his cock twitched to life between them. "Let's just say I plan on welcoming in the New Year a winner."

Private PROPERTY

Security specialist Jodi Tyler has a great job and a great relationship with her boss, Mark Rodriguez—in the office and in the bedroom. Their casual arrangement is all she wants, and she'd thought it was all Mark wanted too. Right up until she's busted while testing the security of a Lake Arlington mansion. To her surprise, and with the help of the mansion's owner, Sam Watson, Jodi's no-strings affair with Mark is about to become a little more…binding.

Sharing Jodi with his best friend Sam was supposed to be fun. But as the intimate evening progresses, certain feelings come to light, feelings Mark didn't know he had. Feelings he doesn't know what to do about. But Sam does. And he knows exactly what to do about them.

By evening's end, the decisions Mark is forced to make will change everyone's lives. He will either disappoint them all—or claim Jodi as his own private property.

CHAPTER ONE

A deep thrum reverberated through Jodi Tyler's chest and stroked the back of her throat with its raw promise of latent power. The unmistakable growl of a Harley. The sound bounced off the highwalled estate hugging the shores of Lake Arlington, then abruptly stopped.

She lifted the night vision binoculars and peered through the tinted windows of the surveillance van. Nothing. Deciding there was no threat from the road, she swiveled her chair back to the monitors. Her fingers flicked the switches controlling the cameras aimed at the estate. Images flashed across the monitor in rapid succession. They all showed the same thing. Nothing.

So where had the motorcycle gone?

"Must've turned off," she muttered to herself. She grabbed the black T-shirt she'd discarded earlier and blotted the sweat trickling down her neck.

Maybe the pimply teenager three doors up drove a Harley. More likely his mid-life-crisis-aged father, she thought, wiping the perspiration pooled between her breasts.

Being stuck in a stifling black van in Dallas during a heat wave was not her idea of excitement. Especially on her birthday. Which Mark had forgotten.

Or ignored.

After hinting for weeks about how she wanted to spend the night, starting with a romantic dinner at their favorite restaurant, after teasing him about the sexy negligee she'd bought, even after that stupid list of all the sexual fantasies she'd written for him, he'd still gone ahead and arranged for her to penetrate the estate tonight. Tonight!

"If he expects me to be in any sort of romantic mood when I get home, he's got rocks in his head." She plopped down in the chair with a huff. "He can sleep in his own bed tonight. Alone."

She switched the monitor back to the camera aimed

at the Lexus parked in front of the five-car garage. If the assistant kept to her regular schedule—and that woman was punctual to a fault—the car would soon be cruising up the drive. Which meant Jodi'd be out of this Easy-Bake Oven and into the air-conditioned estate to finish this assignment. Then she could go home and shower. Alone.

An insidious thought slithered into her mind, puncturing her self-confidence with an icy-cold needle. *That's what he's planned all along—he's trying to dump you without actually having to say anything.*

No, she thought, shaking her head. Mark doesn't play games like that.

How do you know? the voice whispered. Why else would he arrange for the estate to be penetrated today of all days? He's easing his way out of the affair by pissing you off, hoping you'll dump him first. And don't forget how he insisted either one of you could walk away at any point.

She leaned back in the chair, her arms folded across her chest. Easing out of a relationship had to be better than being dumped by text message the way Todd had done. *"Let's just be friends."*

Friends, my ass.

Would it hurt less than it had when she'd found another woman's bra under Danny's bed and been forced to endure his long, stumbling explanation? *"She's softer, less demanding, you know?"*

Yeah, she knew.

Permanent scars etched her heart after Jace's less-than-flattering comments about her lack of femininity when she'd graduated from the police academy. More fool her, she'd quit the force trying to please that asshole and he'd still dumped her.

Maybe Mark's way of easing out of a relationship *was* better. Maybe it would hurt less. She rubbed the heel of her hand over the ache in her heart. Who was she kidding? Despite agreeing with Mark that the affair wouldn't be long term, she'd fallen in love with him anyway. If he was breaking up with her, she was soon going to feel like her skin had been stripped off layer by layer.

When a branch snapped behind the van, interrupting her pity fest, she grabbed her gun from the console and headed to the driver's seat. There was no way she was going to sit here as a witless target.

"Jodi? Open up, babe, it's me," Mark whispered through the back panel.

Excitement flared in her chest at the sound of his voice. When she realized her heart was racing just from hearing his voice, she silently cursed herself for acting like a bookworm with a serious crush on the quarterback.

"Jodi?" Mark said, a little louder this time. "You okay in there?"

She took her hand off her Glock and, after taking a deep breath, opened the door. A glance around showed no sign of his Humvee—he must have parked it farther down the road and walked up.

"You could have phoned to say you were coming in. I might have shot you." In the groin.

The van dipped when he stepped up into it. His six-foot-two-inch frame filling the narrow confines, he gently closed the door so it wouldn't give away their position. The dragon tattoo on his biceps flexed as he placed a knapsack on the console beside the equipment. Muscles rippled beneath the *Celada Security* logo emblazoned across the chest of his black T-shirt. Muscles she'd felt flex beneath her palms the night before.

Her fingers itched to run themselves through the thick crop of black hair in his Marine high-and-tight.

Normally she didn't go for guys with short hair, but that glistening four-inch-wide pelt reminded her of a mink coat she wanted wrapped around her body. Between her legs.

Get over that desire real fast, she told her fingers. "You're late."

"Got stuck at the lawyers'. There—" He stopped as his eyes adjusted to the gloom, reminding her of what she was—or rather, wasn't—wearing.

Every cell in her body went on high alert, trembled with need and expectation as if he'd touched her wherever he looked.

His grin widened and his chocolate brown eyes glinted. "Is a sports bra and thong the latest fashion for surveillance?"

Jodi flipped him the bird while she searched for the T-shirt she'd discarded.

"It was hot. I stripped down. So bite me," she said, though without the rancor she'd intended.

"Anything you say, babe." He pulled her against him and nipped at her earlobe. "But I fully approve of your outfit. Think I should make it part of the dress code."

"Yeah, that'll go over well." She attempted to maintain her anger. And failed. "Everyone's been dying to see Hector's fat ass in a thong."

When his hands cupped her breasts, Jodi melted into his touch. Magic fingers, she thought, as his thumbs brushed her taut nipples. Was this the last time he'd touch her like this? Or was it just her insecurity making her paranoid?

"Have I told you lately how beautiful you are?" he said, his breath hot on her neck.

The citrus fragrance of his aftershave, and the lack of his usual dark five-o'clock shadow told her he'd recently shaved. His fresh scent reminded her how grungy she felt having been cooped up in over one hundred degree heat all day. It took a charming—or incredibly obtuse—man to tell a woman whose hair clung in damp strands to her neck and probably smelled like the inside of a stable that she was beautiful.

Surely a man planning on dumping her wouldn't be acting like this. Or was he overcompensating?

"The assistant leave yet?" His tongue brushed over her earlobe, sending a shiver down her spine.

"Um…" She struggled to think under the onslaught of sensation. His tongue trailed down her neck, teeth nipped at that spot that made her need him inside her.

What was it about him that made her knees turn to jelly and her insides to liquid heat?

"Babe? Did Ms. Hallquist leave?"

She barely heard him repeat the question when his hand released her breast and moved lower. She forced one eye open and peered over his shoulder at the monitor, verifying the car hadn't moved.

"No, not yet. If she keeps to her usual schedule she should leave in ten minutes. I thought I heard an engine a few moments ago. You see anything on the way in?"

"Nope." He turned her away from the monitor and pushed aside the thin strip of her thong. His fingers—those broad, callused, *talented* fingers—stroked her vulva, sending streaks of pleasure deep inside.

She struggled to maintain focus the way he could. "Must have been… Oh, Mark, yes, right there."

Her legs opened wider under his murmured instructions, while her hands fumbled with the zipper in his blue jeans. Fingers were all very well, but when there was a cock willing and eager to penetrate her—and from the rock-hard erection beneath her palm, he was more than ready—there was no contest. There was a rustle of canvas when he reached behind her, and she wondered what was in the knapsack that he needed at this precise moment.

"Got a present for you." His mouth covered hers, swallowing her squeak of surprise when something hard and cold touched her labia and pressed inward. "Something to keep you on your toes."

A moan left her when the object started vibrating inside her. He had to be kidding!

She reached down to remove the vibrating egg, only to have her wrist circled by his fingers, pulling her hand away.

"Oh no you don't. Leave it in until I take it out myself." An intense look filled his dark eyes, replacing the earlier amusement. He stepped back, all business, and picked up her black twill pants. "Better put these on. The assistant will be leaving soon. Don't forget you have to get through the gate right after she leaves."

"I know the plan." She tugged on her pants, doing her best to ignore the overwhelming need the device was creating. "Do you seriously expect me to break into the house and crack a safe with this damned thing vibrating inside me?"

He flashed a six-megawatt grin. "Yup, I do."

Jodi stuck her tongue out at him. Okay, it was childish, but she hated that he'd got her so hot and bothered and then wouldn't let her come. Until she noticed the bulge in his pants. Proving that despite Mark's business-like demeanor, he was just as horny.

"We've got a few minutes before Ms. Hallquist leaves." She trailed a finger down his chest, slid her hand between them and rubbed his erection, intent on torturing him and silencing her insecurities. "You must be aching as bad as I am. No use both of us being unfulfilled all night."

His grin fading, Mark flipped a switch on the remote. The vibrations ceased within her, leaving her with a completely unsatisfied pussy. Damn it, she needed to finish what he'd started.

"Look, babe, I know you wanted to celebrate, but the owner insisted it be today. And since you're our best at infiltration…" He tucked the remote into his shirt pocket then lifted her hands in his.

At least he'd remembered her birthday.

When he pressed his lips against her knuckles, her insecurity crawled back under its rock. Hopefully forever.

"I'd still rather have you inside me than this vibrator."

He chuckled and kissed her fingers again. "I know.

So would I. But we don't have time."

"So why are you insisting I keep it in?"

He let her hands drop and cradled her head to his shoulder briefly. "Just for fun. Besides, you're always practicing cracking those safes wearing headphones, listening to loud music and street sounds. So think of my present as just another distraction, something to add to the challenge."

She relented. A little. There were worse ways to be distracted—like having firecrackers or guns aimed at you—both of which had been done to her in the past. His professionalism had attracted her to him in the first place; it wasn't right that she snark about it now, she supposed. Besides, what could be more exciting than breaking into a house, knowing you could get caught, a vibrator your lover had placed deep inside arousing every fiber of your being? By night's end, she'd be so horny, so desperate for him, he could fuck her in the middle of Dealey Plaza at high noon and she wouldn't deny him.

She bent over to pick up her T-shirt, making sure Mark had a really good look at her butt. Might as well give him something to think about while she was away.

"You got the letter I'm supposed to leave in the

safe?" The shirt muffled her voice as she pulled it over her head.

He held up a sealed envelope. "Right here."

She grabbed the envelope and shoved it in her pocket. "You sure the owner hasn't upgraded the system? Or tipped the current security company off?"

"Nah, I have his word that if you crack the safe tonight, I'll have a signature on a contract at our lunch tomorrow. And then I can concentrate on the merger." Mark perched on the edge of the console and folded his arms. A smug look on his face told her he expected her to encounter no problems.

Yet for all his confidence in her, the envelope weighed a ton in her pocket. "Mark, are you sure you want to sell out? You've worked so hard making Celada the top security firm in Texas—you can't just hand over the reins to some stranger, even if he was your old college buddy. You love running your own company too much to see it gobbled up by Hauberk Security."

He grabbed her hand and tugged until she stood between his legs. "It's just a merger, babe, not a complete takeover. I've told you I'll continue to run ops this side of the Mississippi, and Sam will manage everything to the east from D.C. We'll both have to agree on any major decision, each with an equal say."

"And if you can't agree?"

"It'll work out. Trust me." His hand cupped her buttock and squeezed as he glanced at the monitor behind her. "Time to move, babe. Ms. Hallquist is driving toward the gate."

He couldn't have staged a better way to avoid the subject if he'd planned it.

After pulling on a pair of surgical gloves, Jodi picked up the two-way headset and tucked it around her ear. "Give me a sound check, will you?"

Mark flipped on the microphone to the radio, and whispered something in Spanish.

Shivers flared down her spine and sent a bolt of heat into her core. "One of these days I'm going to take Spanish lessons. What did you say this time?"

"I promised to tie your hands behind your back and make you get on your knees. Then I said I'm going to put my dick in your mouth until I spew come down your throat."

Grabbing the back-door latch, Jodi pressed her knees together as her pussy clamped around the egg lodged high inside. "If you'd let Javier do this job the way I'd suggested, I'd be on my knees in a heartbeat. But since you didn't, I guess you'll have to keep dreaming."

"Maybe. Maybe not." He winked and tossed her a black knit cap. "Forget something?"

With a muttered curse about wool caps and Texas heat, Jodi tucked her hair beneath the cap's edges. Once Mark had flicked off the van's dome light, she eased the door open. As she squeezed through the narrow opening, branches scraped against the door's paint job and tugged at her thin black cotton shirt.

Headlights slanted up the curving driveway, backlighting the ornate wrought-iron gates that creaked as they swung open.

"Right on time. Someone needs to teach you there's safety in unpredictability, lady," she murmured.

The sleek dark blue Lexus drove through the gates and turned right.

"Show time, babe," Mark said over the headset.

Heart thumping, Jodi slid in through the gates as the motor whirred, jumping only slightly when the gate clicked shut behind her.

Keeping to the shadows cast by the half-moon, Jodi crept down the long driveway toward the sprawling three-story Tudor mansion. She skirted the massive garage, then followed the path around back and stopped by the first French door. Whatever security expert designed the current system hadn't insisted that a deadbolt be installed on this one. Or the installers had missed it. And that was the reason she—no, she reminded herself, Mark's company—was going to prove they were the best security firm in Texas.

She pulled out the thin strip of plastic she had tucked in the pouch on her belt and shoved it between the jamb and the latch. Seconds later, she straightened and opened door.

As she'd expected, a red light flashed in the security panel beside the door. She punched in the number she'd memorized and breathed a sigh of relief when the light turned a steady green. They hadn't changed the security code since she'd reconnoitered. Another point for her report.

"I'm in," she whispered, knowing Mark was listening in the van. She wiped the sweat from the back of her neck, angling her head to catch the cool breeze rushing through the air-conditioning vent.

"You never told me how you got the security code," Mark said through the earpiece as she headed through the empty room toward the center hallway.

"I have my secrets," she taunted. That weekend

she'd bribed a maid to call in sick so she could fill in had paid off—even if it meant she'd had to scrub toilets. The work hadn't really been hard—the new owner had only furnished four rooms so far, so there'd not been much to clean.

A smile tugging at her lips, Jodi paused at the door to the office, ensuring it was empty. Moonlight streamed between the heavy curtains that flanked the French doors and across the floor in a rectangular pattern, slanting up the bookcases lining the walls. The red power light on the cordless phone reflected in the brass base of the banker's lamp on the desk. Assured she was alone, she walked confidently toward the desk.

"The safe's in the floor behind the desk," Mark reminded her. "Figure you've got less than an hour to crack the safe, leave the envelope and get out before the next patrol cruises by."

She rolled her eyes. Cruise was right—that's all the minimum-wage cop wannabees currently providing security did for their visual inspection. Her van had been parked in the area for a week now and they hadn't slowed down enough to read her license plate or check why she was there.

She pushed the leather office chair aside and knelt

on the hardwood floor, inhaling a whiff of lemon furniture polish. The very same polish she'd applied on the weekend. Reaching beneath the desk, her fingers found the latch that would free the panel hiding the safe. Her breath left her with a whoosh when she heard the audible click.

"Got it!" she whispered, pumping her fist in the air. Now the real fun began.

Still on her knees, she reached down and swung open the square section of floor concealing the safe. A chuckle escaped her. She'd never bothered to tell Mark that during her stint as a replacement maid, she'd been assigned to dust this room. Or that she'd discovered the safe's combination on the flip side of the leather blotter.

"Hey, Mark, start the timer—I'll bet I can have this baby cracked in under three minutes."

Mark's low chuckle reverberated in her ear. "Two. Loser gets tied up and spanked."

Jodi's butt tightened. Spanking usually meant Mark was in the mood for ass play. Maybe she should deliberately take four minutes. No, she thought with wicked delight as she glanced at her latex covered fingers, it was time Mark got a taste of his own medicine.

"Then drop your pants, big boy, and show me your sweet ass, 'cause you're going to get a whoopin' tonight."

Clenching her penlight between her teeth, she leaned over the dial of the old-fashioned safe. Then jumped when the egg started to vibrate deep inside her.

Sonuvabitch. She stopped herself from screeching. She'd completely forgotten the damned thing. Her nipples hardened into swollen buds rubbing against her cotton T-shirt while her pussy throbbed in time with the vibrations.

No way was she going to let Mark win this bet. Ignoring the vibrator as best she could, she carefully turned the dial clockwise to the first number. One-and-a-half-turns counterclockwise to the second number. Clockwise again. Click. Grinning, she checked her watch.

"Mark, your ass is going to be sore tomorrow," she whispered.

A quick tug on the handle opened the safe. Her penlight's thin beam of light illuminated a thick rope of gold with a massive ruby pendant resting upon a black velvet-covered board. A set of dangly earrings that matched the pendant and several diamond-encrusted bracelets winked back at her. A fortune in easily fenced gems and the idiot had left the combination to the safe where anyone could find it.

Shaking her head at the owner's stupidity, she pulled out the envelope. Then froze when the sliver of light from the French door lengthened, slid beneath the desk and over the safe.

She peered beneath the knee space under the desk. The moonlight outlined the shape of a dark figure shutting the doors.

"Under two minutes, Mark, I win," she announced as she crawled from beneath the desk. She straightened and smiled, expecting Mark to flash that sexy smile of his. She was so ready to fuck him, to have him ram his cock deep into her.

But her smile froze when the intruder took a step into the room and the moonlight gleamed off his head. His *shaved* head.

Not Mark.

"Welcome to my parlor, said the spider to the fly."

CHAPTER TWO

A sudden blaze of light blinded her. Halogen lights glared on the open safe, on the desk. On her.

On him.

A good four inches taller than Mark, the intruder must have weighed at least fifty pounds more, every ounce pure muscle. He looked like he'd stepped out of the Matrix in a dark silk shirt that outlined every bulging muscle in his massive shoulders. While his shaved head gleamed, a day's worth of stubble shadowed his heavy jaw. Beneath thick dark brows and darker eyes, his nose had a bump as if it had been broken, possibly several times. Leather pants clung like a second skin, accentuating the bulging package at the juncture of his legs. Everything about him screamed strength and power.

"If you're fixin' to tell me you're doin' some window-shoppin', this store is closed." He spoke in a slow southern drawl, nothing like Mark's sexy accent.

Her heart rate skyrocketed to triple digits as adrenaline catapulted through her system; sweat slickened the inside of her gloves. Why hadn't Mark warned her that someone was on the grounds?

"You're trespassin' on private property, sweet pea." His deep voice resonated through her chest, its slow cadence drumming a prisoner to the gallows.

Confidence wrapped itself around him in a comfortable cloak. Something in the way he held himself told her not to let his casual pose deceive her. He looked like he could have played defensive end for the NFL and would relish the opportunity to tackle her.

Jodi stared at the inky darkness behind him, hoping he hadn't brought backup. When no one else appeared, her heart rate decreased. Slightly.

"You the owner?" she asked, pleased that her voice didn't betray her anxiety. Or the fact that her pussy was throbbing from the egg still vibrating deep inside her.

"If you belonged here, you'd know who the owner

was."

Did that mean he *was*? Or he wasn't?

She'd checked the names of the cleaning staff personally but couldn't remember anyone of his age or description. The property had been registered under a numbered corporation, and while Mark had met with the owner in person, he hadn't mentioned the man—or woman's name, Jodi amended to be fair.

Jodi lifted her chin, forced her voice to remain steady. "I'm with Celada Security. We've been approached about upgrading the security on this place. Part of the proposal included an agreement that we would breach the perimeter. So here I am—living proof of how pathetic the current system is."

She pulled the envelope from her pocket and held it out, along with her identification. "Here, this'll prove what I'm saying is true."

Goliath plucked the envelope from her hand and tossed it on the desk. "Anyone could have written that letter. It don't prove a damned thing."

He reached into his pocket. Oh my God, he was armed! And she'd left her gun in the van. How could she have been so stupid?

Her mouth pulled a Sahara Desert as her gaze darted toward the door. It couldn't be more than four feet away. She could make it through and be halfway down the hall while he was still rounding the desk. If she could find some way to stop him following her, she might have a better chance of escaping. She inched closer to the doorway, trying hard not to be obvious.

"Ah, now, don't make me chase you. I may be big, but I'm fast." Instead of the knife or gun she was expecting, he pulled out a fat cigar and stuck it in his mouth, held a match to it. "And I guarantee I'll enjoy catchin' you."

An icy lump settled into her stomach as she realized that Mark hadn't responded. She eyed the door again, judging her chances, then glanced at the desk seeking a letter opener or something she could use as a weapon. Maybe a solid thump to his head with the brass banker's lamp would slow him down.

"Relax, sweet pea, I'm not goin' to hurt you." Smoke wreathed his head as he drew on the cigar then carefully placed the cigar in the ashtray beside the lamp. "Much."

Trying to anticipate what his next move might be, Jodi watched him like a mouse eyed a cat. A really hungry cat.

Before she had time to get away, he'd rounded the

desk in a graceful move that belied his size. He crowded her against the wall, his body a furnace wrapped in leather and silk.

She craned her neck up to meet his gaze, and revised her approximation of his height. He had to be at least six foot five. But she'd been right about him being pure muscle.

"Dangerous business, breakin' into private property. Even more dangerous when it's mine."

Mine? Jodi narrowed her eyes. He *was* the owner? So why didn't he just acknowledge that he'd hired the firm to expose the estate's weak spots? What was his game?

"You get a rush breakin' into other people's places? Thwarting their security?"

He grabbed her hand and held it flat against his groin. Against the enormous hard-on straining the buttoned fly. "Do you feel what capturing a trespasser does for me?"

His gaze flicked down her body as his grin widened. "You're a little skinny for my tastes but I'll bet you're a real wildcat in bed. We're gonna have a lot of fun tonight, we are. I can't wait to bury my cock in your sweet pussy." He dipped his head until his mouth was beside her ear and whispered, "I'll bet you're already dripping wet, aren't you?"

She snatched her hand away and dragged in a breath, forcing air into her too-tight lungs as she memorized his features. "It'll be a cold day in hell before that happens, asshole. Now back off before I shove your dick down your throat."

His lips twitching as if he wanted to laugh, he took a half step back, but not enough for her to sidle past him. "I'd rather shove it down yours."

"Just read the letter. It'll prove I'm who I say I am, and am doing what we were hired to do. Or if you don't believe the letter is legit, call Mr. Rodriguez yourself."

She rattled off Mark's cell phone number while wondering why he still hadn't responded over the headset.

When he unfolded the paper and started reading it, his eyebrows arched and his lips compressed into a controlled smirk.

"*My Sexual Fantasies.*" His eyes flickered up and he grinned while Jodi narrowed her eyes, trying to figure his game. "Sounds like an interesting letter your boss wrote, Miz Tyler."

Just what she needed—a smart-ass.

"Just read the damned thing," she ground out.

"I *am* reading." He unfolded the paper again. "My Sexual Fantasies. One, to try anal sex. Two, I want to be fucked by Mark while tied up and blindfol—"

What the hell? Jodi snatched the paper from him with a gasp and stared in horror at the list she had jokingly made for Mark.

"This is a mistake," she stammered. "It was supposed to be the letter Mark—I mean Mr. Rodriguez had written explaining exactly how we'd breached security and his recommendations to make the estate safer."

He chuckled and looked over his shoulder to the French doors. "Is that what it was supposed to say, *Mr. Rodriguez*?"

Jodi followed his gaze. The knapsack at his feet, Mark leaned against the doorframe, thumbs tucked into the belt of his jeans that rode low over his hips.

Tension drained like a plug had been pulled, Jodi sagged against the wall. Until she realized Mark was not out of breath, nor was he treating the other man with caution. In fact, he was downright relaxed and smiling. She straightened, vowing vengeance for his screwup with the list. And for not letting her know he was all right. *And* for not warning her someone was about to walk in on her. Not to mention the vibrator still buzzing away deep inside, driving her insane.

"Will you please explain that I work for you, *Mr. Rodriguez?*" she gritted out, her hands curled into fists. "And will you please turn *it* off?"

"Sam?" Mark arched an eyebrow at her captor.

"I'd rather leave it on," Sam grumbled, but he reached into his pocket and the vibrator immediately ceased.

"*You* had the…?" Jodi spluttered when he held the remote up for her to see. "But Mark had… Mark, what the hell is going on here?"

"Jodi Tyler, I'd like you to meet Sam Watson."

Sam Watson? *As in the owner of Hauberk Security and Mark's college buddy*? Jodi closed her mouth when she realized her jaw was hanging open. Was this some sort of joke?

"So is this really your place, or are you checking me out to make sure I meet your company's qualifications?"

"Yup, place is all mine." He smiled as he picked up the cigar, his gaze flicking over her again. "As for checking you out, there ain't a man alive who could fail to admire your…assets."

Annoyed at being held captive by the man who

would soon be her new boss, she placed her hands flat on Sam's chest and pushed. And failed to budge him at all.

"Since you own one of the biggest security firms on the east coast, you obviously don't need Mark to upgrade your security—so why have me break in? Oh, and in case you haven't heard, there's a law about sexual harassment of employees. So you'd better have one damned good lawyer."

Sam's eyes widened; he quickly stepped back, letting Mark take his place.

"Relax, babe." Mark rubbed her shoulders in a move meant to pacify her but she batted them away.

Jodi shoved the paper in Mark's face. It was either that or kick him in the groin. "This list was supposed to be just between us. How could you humiliate me like this?"

Mark cleared his throat and cursed softly in Spanish. "I'm sorry, babe, I wanted to surprise you for your birthday—you know, so we can cross the rest of those items off your list. I thought it would be funny. Sort of an icebreaker."

"Funny?" She thumped her fist into his shoulder. "You have a twisted sense of humor. Besides, what could possibly be on there that you'd need to show to a perfect stranger?"

Sam waved his cigar toward the paper that was now a crumpled ball in her fist. "You might wanna refresh your memory and read number six there. Ol' Mark here's asked me to help fulfill that particular fantasy."

With a growing dread, she scanned the list, her eyes widening.

6. I'd like to have a ménage with Mark and another man that we could trust.

CHAPTER THREE

A ménage? While she'd secretly fantasized about that particular scenario, she'd not realized she'd written it down, nor that Mark wouldn't consult her on who the third person might be.

Wait a minute! This whole thing had been a setup? From the first time Mark mentioned the owner's challenge to break through the current security, to how he'd manipulated the roster so she pulled the majority of the surveillance? And this morning, when she'd tried to finagle the evening off so they could spend her birthday together, he'd insisted she be the one in the van…that she be the one infiltrating the estate. It had all been a lie?

"So you've been planning this for…what? A month now?"

"Yup." Mark wore a smug, satisfied smile, like the proverbial cat who'd captured the canary—and still had yellow feathers clinging to his mouth. "Fooled you, didn't I? Happy birthday, babe."

Letting out a small screech, Jodi tore the list into pieces and flung them in Mark's face. She ripped off her knit cap and clutched a hank of her still-sweaty hair, holding it out at right angles. "So you made me spend twelve hours cooped up in a van until I smell like I spent all day in a swamp and thought that would put me in the mood for sex? And not just sex, but for fucking my future boss?"

"Told you you might want to rethink the idea of just springin' it on her, ol' buddy," Sam murmured.

She continued as if she hadn't been interrupted, poking Mark in the chest with one finger. "Did you think I might not like to have a say in who is the third? Or that it might affect how *Mr. Watson* judges me in the future?"

"Two-way street there, sugar. You don't need to worry about me judgin' you for your sexual preferences if you don't judge me. An' I told Mark I wasn't gonna participate unless you were willin'." Sam tamped the cigar out in the ashtray once more, his face a carefully blank mask. "Guess I got my answer. No harm, no foul."

"Sam, wait," Mark said, running a hand over his thick strip of hair. "Look, Jodi, maybe I should have let you in on it from the get-go, but if you remember I promised I'd try to fulfill all your fantasies. Which is what I'm doing."

She attempted to resist him when he tugged her close, refusing to look at him. He wrapped his arms around her, cradling her until she melted against him.

"Babe, I trust Sam more than I'd trust any other man with you." He pulled back and looked at her with narrowed eyes. "Or did you have someone else in mind?"

"No," she sighed. "I can't think of anyone else."

"Tell you what," Sam said. "Why don't you two take a couple minutes and discuss it without me around? Go on up to the master bedroom and use that whirlpool tub big enough for six, or take a shower or something while you make up your mind. You might remember it since you did such a good job cleaning it when you played maid on the weekend—*Bianca*."

Jodi winced at Sam's reminder of her subterfuge.

Mark folded his arms across his chest and raised one eyebrow. Though he was attempting to be stern, the edges of his lips twitched as if he were trying to stop smiling. "I wondered how you cracked the security code."

"Girl's gotta have some secrets," she muttered.

"I'll be back directly." Sam picked up his cigar and stuck it in his mouth. "If you decide to stay, pick up the phone and dial pound-one-two."

He stopped in the doorway and winked. "Oh, and *Bianca*? Call me if you need any help scrubbin' up. I'm real good with a loofah."

MARK CLOSED THE BATHROOM DOOR BEHIND THEM, watching as Jodi wandered over to the long cherrywood vanity and stood in front of the gold-tapped white marble sinks, her lips pursed. She'd been quiet while she'd led him out of the study and up the stairs. He noticed she hadn't taken him to the master bedroom with the massive tub Sam had mentioned. Obviously she still wasn't comfortable with the idea of Sam joining them.

He should have at least given her a choice of who should be the "other man". And he should have realized she'd have wanted to primp a bit before the main event. *Way to go, Rodriguez.*

"We don't have to have the threesome. Just say the word and we'll go home and I'll never mention the list again."

Frowning, Jodi pulled the headset from her ear and set it on the white marble counter, watching it spin as it settled into place. Her tongue darted out, licked her top lip before she looked up into the mirror and met his gaze. "I know you meant well…"

Mark hesitated before voicing a concern that had raised its ugly head when he'd seen her reaction to Sam reading her fantasies aloud. "Jodi? Those things on the list—the bondage, the anal sex? Were they really things you wanted to try? Or were they just things you thought would keep me happy?"

Color rose up her neck and into her cheeks. He wondered if she realized she was wringing her hands.

Her tongue slid across her full upper lip again. "Some of them were."

"Which means some of them weren't." He crossed the room in three strides, tugged her by the hips until she rested against him. "Why did you feel you needed to put things on the list if you didn't want to try them? You know I'd never force you to do something you didn't want to do."

"Well, some of them I didn't know I wanted to do until we did them. Like you fucking my ass, but then…" One shoulder lifted as her chin went down along with her lids, and the pink in her cheeks brightened to deep red flags. "I liked it."

Mark barked a laugh that echoed around the room. "Liked it? Talk about an understatement. I thought the neighbors were going to call the cops the first time we did it at your place, you screamed so loud when you came."

She wrapped her arms around his neck and tilted her head back up so he could finally see her eyes were filled with a mixture of embarrassment and mirth. "And the night you tied me up was a real turn-on too. I had no idea I was such a control freak and that letting go would be so enjoyable."

Her answer let him relax. Her headstrong intensity when she'd stood up to clients—and him on occasion when their opinions had differed—was something that had first attracted him to her. He wanted to savor the fierce passion that simmered beneath her cool exterior. Forever.

He kissed the tip of her nose as he reached down and tugged her T-shirt over her head. "You don't have to decide right now. Think about it while you take your shower."

She stepped out of her pants, leaving her once again in her thong and bra. He shifted so he stood behind her and pulled her against him. He looked at the image of them in the mirror and wondered why she—one of the most beautiful and intelligent operatives he'd ever met—had chosen him. And why she'd agreed to his no-attachments stipulation. He marveled at how her hair seemed to glow in the vanity lights. At how her full lips, slightly parted, urged him to kiss her. And how the light skin of her breasts contrasted with the tanned skin of his forearm cradling them. His dick firmed at the memory of three nights before when he'd come between them.

Though she'd never said a word of complaint, he knew his sexual demands had challenged her. He'd hated the thought that she might have done things she hadn't wanted to simply to please him. Those idiots who she'd dated before had her convinced she wasn't desirable. Damned if he'd let her think he thought the same thing.

"Open your eyes, babe."

The lights caught the sheen filling her eyes as she met his gaze in the mirror.

"Do you see what I see?" When she shook her head and tried to look away, he dipped his head and placed his cheek against hers to force her to continue looking in the mirror. "I see a beautiful woman with hair that's as bright as sunshine and soft as silk. I see dark grey eyes filled with love that brings me to my knees every time you look at me. I see full lips that make me hard just thinking of them wrapped around my dick."

Her pink tongue darted out to lick her top lip and her hips swiveled, pressing his erection into the crack of her ass.

"You drive me crazy when it licks my balls, and swirl your tongue along my shaft as you suck me deep into your throat."

He cupped her breast, his thumb rubbing her nipple until it hardened. "I see a beautiful woman, with breasts begging to be kissed. I see nipples as ripe as berries that I want to suckle from them all night long."

His hand drifted over the smooth planes of her stomach to the thin triangle of hair at the juncture of her legs. "Full, pouty lips down here, too."

Jodi chuckled. When his fingers pushed aside the thin fabric and stroked, her chuckles changed to moans.

"And between those sweet lips of yours, there's a passage so tight and responsive I swear I lose my mind every time my cock slides into you."

Her head fell back against his shoulder and her hips rotated, betraying her insatiable need. He slid his hand over her hip and clasped one of her tight cheeks. "You've got the most beautiful ass any man could hope to see. Let alone fuck."

She murmured something about it being too big so he caught her gaze in the mirror, held it.

"Stop putting yourself down. You're beautiful." He released her and lightly slapped her butt. "Now you have your shower and decide what you want to do tonight. No pressure, all right?"

When he began to step back, she stopped him, cupping his head with her palm, pulling him down so she could kiss him. Her lips brushed against his in a soft promise that quickly turned so hot he would have sworn the mirrors should have been coated with steam.

"I may need some help washing my back," she whispered, her breath warm against his cheek.

CHAPTER FOUR

Wearing a fresh set of clothes Mark had stuffed into the backpack, Jodi trailed him into the study. The only light in the room was provided by the green-shaded bankers' lamp on the desk. The floor panel once again concealed the safe, and the pieces of the list she'd scattered had disappeared. Sam stood in the shadows, his back to the room, staring out the door.

When Mark cleared his throat, Sam turned and tilted his head. "Let me assure you again, Jodi, that whatever your decision is, it'll not change anything between us in the future, especially in the office. I don't want you to feel pressured into anything tonight. Plus tonight is a one-time-only offer. When you walk away, whether anything happens or not, we will never discuss it again. That clear?"

Thoughts bounced randomly in her brain like popcorn in hot oil. Was she so boring in bed that this was what Mark needed to get excited? Would he walk away completely if she turned him down? And if she didn't, what would he demand next? An orgy, with her the main attraction?

No. Mark had also said if she turned his offer down, he'd never discuss it again. Two men at the same time. Could she live with herself if she agreed to Mark's plan?

She glanced down at the bulge between Sam's legs. And that was when he *wasn't* aroused.

Could she live with herself if she *didn't* agree? Or would she forever regret passing up the opportunity?

"So can we help you check another fantasy off your list?" Mark asked.

He moved close enough that she could feel the heat radiating from him, could smell the last lingering scents of herself on his breath. "Picture it, babe. Two mouths, two tongues to lick your breasts, to lap at your sweet pussy. Four hands to hold you, caress you, pleasure you." He pressed her hand flat against his groin, letting her feel his arousal. "And two cocks at your command."

As she watched, the bulge at Sam's groin grew, straining the leather taut. Heat rushed through her, and her eyelids grew heavy at the imagined sensation of the two men kissing her breasts; her pussy pulsed at the idea of being watched fucking Mark. Or Mark watching her being fucked by Sam. She licked her lips, imagining herself taking his cock into her mouth while Mark rammed into her from behind.

"I think…I think I'd like to stay. But I want you both to agree that if I decide to stop, you will."

"Of course," Sam quickly agreed. "Pick a safe word and we'll stop whatever we're doing the moment you say it."

Excitement mixed with trepidation slithered under her skin like an electric current.

"My safe word is…broccoli."

Both men exhaled as if they'd been holding their breath.

"Broccoli it is," Sam said. "Now before we get started, I just need your assurance about a coupla things."

"What?"

"Do you trust Mark's choice in me as the third? Do you trust that I'll not hurt you or use anything that happens tonight against either of you?"

Her shoulders relaxed. She answered quickly, "Yes, I trust Mark's judgment. I mean, I trust you won't hurt me."

"Good." Sam walked over to her and held out one hand, as the other reached behind his back.

Smiling, she extended hers, expecting him to shake on their agreement. He took it, then immediately clamped a leather restraint around her wrist with his other hand. She let out a squeak and jumped back only to run into Mark's hard chest.

Sam's brows drew together until they met in the middle. "You wimping out already? Or have you forgotten item two on your list?"

Item two? To be tied up. Yeah, to be tied up by *Mark*, she wanted to tell him. Her lips parted as she began to object, then she closed them firmly. No, she had the safe word. Let's see where this led. She squared her shoulders and looked him straight in the eye. Bring it on. "You just surprised me, that's all."

"Standard procedure to cuff a burglar," Sam said.

All her apprehension fled as she realized the nature of the game they were going to play.

He held up a second wrist cuff and tossed it to Mark. "Why don't you do the other one? There's a clasp on 'em so they'll snap together just like handcuffs."

Mark bound her left wrist then pulled her hands behind her and snapped the cuffs together. He pulled on her arms, ensuring she couldn't free herself and grunted in satisfaction. "I think you should pat her down. You know, to ensure she's not concealing any weapons?"

Wrapping one arm across her chest, Mark held her firmly against him. His breath blew hot in her ear, down her neck, sending a blast of heated blood through her belly to pool between her legs. While he'd often handcuffed her in private, she nearly whimpered in excitement at being held captive in front of a stranger. Her nipples hardened when his palm cupped her breast, squeezed. Hard. A moan escaped her, and she squirmed against the engorged length pressing into the cleft of her ass.

Her knees trembled as Sam's huge hands patted up her calves, her thighs, swept up her side, lingered over her breasts. He tweaked her nipples, and his lids drooped over his dark eyes.

"You broke into this place, you need to be punished. Don't you?"

"Yes," she whispered. "Punish me."

CHAPTER FIVE

A tornado whirled through her when Sam's large hand stroked her mound through the thin fabric of her pants, igniting fires in their wake. Jodi groaned, arched her hips into the broad fingers.

"She's so hot steam's risin' off her," Sam said with a chuckle.

From Mark's harsh breath beside her ear, and his rigid arm muscles, Jodi could tell he was not unaffected. The tension in his voice removed all doubt. "She likes relinquishing control. Most times."

Sam leaned down to her, the rough stubble of his beard scraping the tender skin of her cheek.

"Gorgeous." Sam stroked a strand of hair that curled

over her ear. "It's like silk."

He stepped closer, ground his erection into her mound as he licked a spot just beneath her ear, the unexpected contact making her jump. Another moan escaped her at being sandwiched between the two aroused men. "Time for your punishment."

The leather of Sam's pants creaked as he pulled away from her and knelt in front of the credenza. He opened a cabinet door and removed a box, flipping open the lid. As he poked through it, Jodi strained to see what it contained, but Mark held her firmly in place.

Sam held up two thick leather collars, one encrusted with bright stainless steel spikes, the other glittering with what had to be rhinestones and rubies. There were so many they couldn't be the real thing. Could they? Besides who used real gems on bondage devices?

"Which do you prefer to restrain our suspect?"

Mark chose the spiked leather collar and carefully wrapped it around her neck.

Sam frowned. "We need a leash for that collar." He pulled out a silver chain and snapped the clasp over the ring on the collar. With a wide smile, he ceremoniously handed the chain to Mark. "Just to make sure she doesn't run away. Can't say we lost our suspect, now, can we?"

After rummaging through the box once more, Sam pulled out two matching anklets. Cool hands pushed her pants halfway up her calves, broad calloused fingers stroked her bared legs before removing her boots and socks and setting them aside.

A shiver raced from her throat and settled in her breasts at the warmth of Mark's hands compared to Sam's cool touch. Soon she'd have both hands touching her, fondling her, dominating her.

"Such pretty feet," he murmured as he fastened matching leather restraints around her ankles.

"What are you going to do with me?" Her voice was breathless as she ran through the various possible punishments the two men might have devised. Would they interrogate her using the good cop/bad cop technique? Would she get to go down on one while the other fucked her, just like she'd fantasized?

"Ah, sweet pea, I'm not gonna tell you—that would ruin the anticipation now, wouldn't it? And just so you can't cheat and see what we've got planned..." Sam stuck his hand in his pocket, retrieving a blindfold.

He placed it over her eyes and tied it in place, extinguishing all light. "You see anything?"

"No."

"You wouldn't lie to me now, would you?"

She shook her head, almost losing her balance in the process.

Mark grabbed one elbow, Sam the other, as they walked her out of the office and into the hall. They turned in the opposite direction she'd come and walked what felt like the length of the thickly carpeted hall before they stopped. There was a whirring noise and they walked her forward a few paces onto a tiled surface then stopped, turned her around. The floor lurched beneath her feet.

The elevator the previous owner had installed.

But was she going up or down? Up, she decided.

The motion stopped, followed by the metallic chime of the doors sliding open. They led her out and to the left. Disoriented because of the blindfold, she tried to recall the floor plan she'd studied. They had to be in the master bedroom. She frowned when she heard the sound of a pocket door scraping in its tracks right in front of her and then was led forward. The thick carpet cushioning her bare feet changed to cool tile. They were taking her into the bathroom?

"Watch your step, Jodi," Mark urged. "We're going

downstairs."

Downstairs? There was nothing in the blueprints about stairs off the master bathroom—and why would they have taken her up in the first place? She slid her foot along the tile and tentatively felt in front of her until she found the step.

"And again." Then a third step, and a fourth. After fourteen they finally stopped on a concrete floor.

"Mark?" she whispered, suddenly unsure of her decision.

"It's all right, babe. Sam's had a safe room built into the house—we're going to be using it tonight." Mark rubbed her arm as something metallic hissed and creaked.

The sound changed, got hollow as they led her into what she could only guess was a larger room.

"Hit the light switch there, will you, Mark?"

Light glimmered from beneath the edges of the blindfold.

"Lift your foot and step up." Sam took her arm and lead her a few more paces. "There you go."

Jodi took a deep breath, forcing herself to relax. Bound and blindfolded, led to a room that didn't exist? So far, none of this had been how she'd pictured her fantasy. And yet…it was exactly right.

After Mark released the clasp fastening her wrists together, he massaged her shoulders. "Wait'll you see this place, babe. We're going to have a blast."

"All set?" Sam said after a few moments.

"Okay."

As one, they lifted her arms as high as her shoulders. Something cold and hard encircled her wrists. Handcuffs? There was a metallic clinking, then their hands dropped away, leaving her arms suspended in mid-air. A fresh shiver of anticipation crawled up her spine and under the skin of her arms.

"Can you move?" Mark said from just in front of her.

She pulled on the restraints but her bonds didn't budge. Hopefully they wouldn't leave her here too long—the blood would drain out of her hands.

Something cold and hard—metallic—touched her right biceps. After a slight tug, it slid to her shoulder and along the seam to her neck. The fabric slithered down her front, baring one breast. She could feel her nipple puckering under the blast of air-conditioned air from a vent above her.

They were *cutting* her clothes off her? Thank God

Mark had brought one of the company tees rather than something from her closet.

The sensation was repeated on her left arm. Soon her top slithered down her belly and came to rest on her bare feet.

"You have real pretty tits, sweet pea. Your nipples are like ripe berries waiting to be plucked."

"She thinks they're too small," Mark said with a chuckle.

"And I'm sure Mark's told you that more than a mouthful's wasted."

Heat rose up her neck. Being naked was never a hang-up for her, but being naked in front of another man while Mark watched. Would he be jealous? Or did he not feel the way she would if he was viewing another woman? Maybe he didn't love her the way she loved him.

A tongue swept over her right nipple, but she couldn't tell whose. Warm breath moved across her cleavage, then lips laved her left breast, teeth nipping lightly. "Taste as sweet as berries too."

Fire swirled in her breast and shot straight to her pussy when she realized it was Sam touching her, kissing her. It shouldn't feel so good to know another man was arousing her when Mark was right there.

Should it?

The cool edge of the knife touched first one hip, then the other, and her pants slid over her ankles.

Two sets of lips kissed her almost reverently—one kissing her belly button, the other feathering down the small of her back.

"You should see how turned on Mark is right now," Sam whispered from behind. "How much he wants you."

Warm lips pressed against the back of her neck as a hand cupped her breast. "Isn't she beautiful, Mark?"

"Oh yeah." Mark's voice sounded strained. "I'm so hard I ache, babe."

"Now be a good little burglar and lift your foot," Sam said from her left side.

The moment she did, he pulled the remnants of her clothes from her ankle.

"Now your right foot," Mark said from that side.

When she put her foot back down on the ground, two sets of hands wrapped gently around her ankles.

"Spread your legs, babe."

They fastened the ankle restraints, leaving her standing spread-eagled, unable to move. A fly captured in a spider's web.

Two sets of hands ran up her calves, her thighs. Fingers parted her cleft, dipped forward into moisture coating her labia, then traced back and circled the tight bud of her rear.

"I'll bet your ass is so tight my dick'll feel like it's been taken to heaven when I'm fucking it," Sam whispered as his finger broached deeper, his breath a warm caress against her ass. A hiss of indrawn breath revealed Mark's location.

The idea of someone else—of Sam—fucking her while Mark watched sent fireballs to every nerve ending in both her pussy and her ass. How could she have considered leaving earlier?

"Punishment time, Jodi," Mark whispered in her ear. Her heart immediately raced as if she'd been running.

A marathon.

Up the side of a mountain.

The sharp whistling sound of…what was that? It reminded her of a whip, or a belt arcing through the air. Her butt tightened at the thought of being paddled or spanked as her punishment.

"Now, sweet pea, we're going to play a game. If you

guess correctly, you get rewarded. If you guess incorrectly, you'll be punished."

"What do I have to do?"

Lips touched hers. Lips tasting of cigar smoke. "You have to guess which one of us—"

"—is doing what to you," Mark finished, nibbling just below her ear.

"Someone's gonna touch you…"

"When whatever they're doing stops you have to say who it was."

They were circling her, trying to confuse her.

"If you get it wrong…"—something whistled through the air, stung her ass in a thin line—"then you'll be punished."

Heat gathered in the cheek where she'd been hit. Mark had only ever used the flat of his hand, but the thin instrument they'd just used focused the sensation, which shot straight to her core. "And if I get it right?"

"Then you'll be rewarded."

"How?"

"You'll find that out when that happens."

"But you have to get one right first, sugar.".

"And to make it a bit more of a challenge for you, your time will be limited." Someone's palm—Mark's she guessed—smacked flat against her ass again, blurring the thin line of heat from the last hit. "Hmm. She liked your riding crop better. You know, I think I might try out some of your toys."

"Be my guest, there's enough to choose from," Sam said with a chuckle.

Jodi wiggled her ass in anticipation.

"Oh, and, Jodi? If you don't answer quick enough, you'll be punished no matter what your answer."

Something rattled, followed by a sharp snap. Was that a...flogger?

"Are you prepared to accept our punishment?" Mark asked.

"Yes." More than ready. Cream leaked down her thigh in a torturous tickle.

Seconds later, a hand caressed her left breast. Cool but gentle fingers tweaked her nipple. She rolled her head back, arching at the sensation when a tongue swirled across her other taut peak, teeth nipping lightly. The hint of cigar wafted up. A smile curled her lips—she would soon find out what her reward would be.

Too soon the touching, the licking, stopped. The sudden lack of contact left her panting, wanting more.

"Time to guess, Jodi," Mark said from her left side.

"Was it me?"

"Or me," Sam whispered from her right side.

A wicked thought occurred to her; she struggled to stop her smile from showing. She enjoyed Mark punishing her, and the anticipation of discovering what rewards they had planned would be that much more intense. Besides she always did prefer being the bad girl to the good.

"Mark."

"Wrong!"

Even though she was expecting it she jumped when the flogger whistled and cracked with a thwack against her tender skin. The heat in her buttocks spread straight to her pussy.

"I'm not sure she thought that a punishment, ol' buddy," Sam said with a chuckle.

A large warm palm flattened over her belly, fingers spread wide, played with her belly button ring. They moved lower, parting her labia. Hot breath tickled her navel when whoever knelt in front of her exhaled. A finger—or was that a thumb?—circled the sensitive bundle of nerves that ached to be touched, slipped around it, below, never satisfying her need.

"Please," she whimpered. She squirmed, trying to

force the digit over that spot.

The movement stopped, the traitorous hand withdrew She jumped when the crop stung her ass again.

"But I haven't guessed yet!"

"You moved. That's against the rules," Mark said from her right.

"You will stand still when we touch you, or we will leave you hanging there and not touch you again," Sam said from her left. "Now tell us who it was who made you so needy?"

She tried to guess who it might have been…

"Tick tock, sweet pea."

…there had been no scent of cigar, no creak of leather…

"Five, four, three—"

"Mark!"

Sam heaved a long sigh, and from the sound, she got the feeling he was shaking his head.

"It wasn't?" Wouldn't she have been spanked for guessing wrong?

"No, you were right, sugar, but I'm disappointed that you've not credited me yet." He let out another dramatic sigh.

"You still owe me a reward," she reminded him.

"You're right. We do."

After a moment, she sensed movement—someone knelt directly in front of her. Warm breath caressed her breast, a tongue swiped over one nipple then drew it into his mouth and began to suckle. One hand caressed her ass, another slipped between her legs. A finger slid inside. A second. Then a third, fucking her until every nerve ending inside her threatened to burst into flame. She nearly cried when they withdrew.

"Let's see what you can earn next," Mark said.

Calloused hands caressed her ass, broad fingers parted her cheeks. A tongue laved from front to back, rimming her.

"Sam."

Someone—Mark? or Sam?—sucked her nipples as a finger trailed through her cream, drew it back along her ass. It circled her tight bud then nudged inside, waiting as her muscles adjusted to the invasion. Her suspicion that it was Sam was confirmed when rough stubble abraded her inner thighs. Sam tongued the throbbing bundle of nerves, then thrust his tongue into her pussy. A second finger joined the first, stretching her ass wider, then both thrust in time with his tongue. Just as she was ready to leap over the edge, the fingers and mouths withdrew.

Shaking with her need, she cried, "No! Please! I need to come."

FIRE LICKED IN MARK'S BELLY, TIGHTENED LIKE A VISE ABOUT HIS CHEST, as he watched Sam laving Jodi's clit with a tenderness he hadn't expected. Watched her arch her back, listened to her unsteady breathing, the breathy moan she made in her pleasure.

What the fuck was going on that he'd resent the hell out of his friend for doing exactly what he'd asked him to do? Damn it, he'd been the one who'd approached Sam and yet now he wanted to pull him off Jodi, to ram his fist into Sam's face.

Sam's gaze flicked over to him, rested briefly on the flogger in his hand. Mark glanced down and realized he'd gripped it so hard his knuckles were white.

When Sam resumed tonguing her glistening pussy, Mark took a step back. Closed his eyes so he wouldn't see how she rotated her hips toward Sam's mouth. Tried to close his ears to the sound of Jodi's soft whimpers.

Whimpers he wanted to be for him. Only him.

"Please," Jodi pleaded. "Please, Sam, please let me come. I really need this."

Mark's teeth ground so hard, he swore sparks would shoot from his mouth. She should be begging *him* to make her come, not Sam. What made him think Jodi was someone he could stand by and watch as someone else fucked her?

He opened his eyes to find Sam picking up the crop he'd set down.

"No moving, remember?" Sam gave Mark a curious look as he snapped the crop across Jodi's ass.

Her thighs quivered as if they tried to close, to press together and ease the ache in her voice.

God, she was so beautiful. So responsive.

Beneath her blindfold, he knew her eyelids would be heavy from sexual arousal. His hand lifted of its own accord, hovered over Jodi's full bottom lip, wanting to stroke it; his body leaned in until he could feel the heat of her body brush his. He wanted to drop to his knees and kiss the taut, budded nipples, hear her beg for more attention. His attention.

He'd go down on her, taste that wonderful cream streaming down her thighs. Suck on her clit, use his fingers against that spot that he knew drove her insane. He'd bring her to orgasm again and again, and each time she'd scream his name. *His* name. No one else's. Ever.

But after he'd gone to Sam and suggested this evening, after he'd convinced Jodi it would be fun, how could he back out? How could he tell Sam to leave? He'd look like a first-class idiot.

"Such a pretty pink ass you've got," Sam said. "And your pussy is so wet it's dripping down your thighs like Niagara Falls. Hey, Mark, hand me that cloth, will you, buddy?"

When Sam's large hand caressed her ass and Jodi moaned her approval, Mark's vision went red.

CHAPTER SIX

ere you go." A dark anger reverberated through Mark's voice, a threatening tone she'd heard only once before—when a suspect had attacked her from behind. She wished she could see his face, see into his eyes and know what he was thinking.

The sound of a scuffle and Mark's explosive "What the fuck!" had her tugging at her restraints but they held fast. Her vulnerability slapped her harder than any flogging she'd had that night, squeezed the breath from her lungs.

Footsteps—shuffling noises, grunts—came from behind her.

"What the fuck are you doing, Watson? Get off me!"

There was a bang as if someone had been shoved into a wall and a rattling noise as something skittered across the floor.

"Mark! Mark?" Her breath came in short, quick gasps while her legs could barely support her. "Mark, what's happening? What's the matter? Sam, what are you doing? Let him go!"

"I'm doing this for your own good, buddy."

"You hurt Jodi, I'll fucking kill you, Watson." The undercurrent of fear in Mark's voice sent ice cubes tumbling down Jodi's spine. "I'll cut off your balls and shove 'em so far down your throat they'll come out your ass."

Flesh smacked on flesh and Sam grunted. "God-damn it, buddy, you're wrigglier than a greased pig. I've just changed up the plan, that's all."

Sam's voice came closer. She pulled back as far as the restraints allowed her, which meant she could barely move.

"Now don't you fuss there, if that boyfriend of yours would just shut his face for a minute, I think you'll both agree to my little change of plan."

Jodi blinked in the light as Sam gently peeled the blindfold from her face.

"It's all right, honey, I'm not going to hurt you. But you'd better slow down your breathin' before you pass out." He cupped her face with his huge hand. "In through your nose and out through your mouth, all right?"

Somewhat dazed that she was trusting him, she followed his direction, forcing air into steel-banded lungs. The trembling in her legs and arms gradually subsided.

"I would never do anything you didn't want me to do, Jodi. I'm going to let you free, but first you have to promise to listen to my proposal, all right?"

"Mark?" she asked, forcing air from her lungs. "What have you done with Mark?"

After a moment's hesitation, Sam moved aside.

Her eyes widened to see Mark lying on a gargantuan bed. Heavy leather straps restrained his arms and legs, spread-eagled until he resembled a prisoner in the dungeon of a medieval castle. Except the bright room she found herself in resembled no medieval castle she'd ever seen.

Mirrors lining the walls and ceiling reflected the bed. Overstuffed multicolored pillows of various shapes were scattered across the floor, dislodged from the bed no doubt by Mark's struggles. A giant flat-screen television loomed at the end of the bed, a second hung over the headboard, yet another was mounted flat within the mirrored ceiling for the ultimate viewing experience from any angle. A leather sling hung in one corner while chairs and a bench had been grouped by a large unlit fireplace. More cushions and wedges covered in leather and velvet and silk were heaped upon them but didn't hide the leather restraints on the arms.

There was no ambiguity about the purpose of the room—it had been designed for every sexual position that she could have dreamed of—and several she couldn't.

Mark glared at their captor as he continued cursing Sam, a look so fierce on his face that Jodi shivered. She'd seen Mark in action, seen how he could take down an armed opponent barehanded. To be chained, pinned, useless would be torture for him. And yet there was something so provocative, so compelling about having Mark bound. Would Sam let her have a say in what directions their games would now take?

"Trust me, Jodi. Please," Sam said quietly. "I'm just changing the original plans Mark and I worked out, that's all. But I think you'll both enjoy what I've got planned."

Mark's scowl darkened. "Just what has that perverted mind of yours dreamed up this time, Watson?"

Sam smiled at Jodi, though a cautious look shadowed his eyes. "He calls *me* perverted after he suggested tonight's entertainment."

His light-hearted gibe belied the worry lines crinkling his forehead, and the way he kept glancing between her and Mark. He obviously wasn't as sure they'd approve of his plan as his tone implied.

"Will you promise that when I let you go, you won't attack me? Will you at least hear me out?"

She caught her bottom lip between her teeth, wondering how to interpret the dark look Mark shot her. He'd arranged the game, he'd trusted Sam. Now it was up to her to trust Mark's judgment.

A slight nod of her head gave him her answer.

"Thank you." Sam knelt beside her and began to unfasten the leather strap attaching her ankle to one of the two posts she'd been tied to. Despite her assurance she'd listen to him, he kept the post between them so she couldn't easily kick him. But then why should he trust her given how he'd betrayed Mark's trust?

AFTER SAM FREED BOTH JODI'S ANKLES, he flipped open the clasp restraining her right arm, took her wrist in his and chafed it between his palms. He freed her left hand, and massaged that wrist too. She glanced down and saw just how huge his hands were as they engulfed her small one, and knew they could snap her bones as easy as a dry twig. Yet he held her so gently she might have been a baby bird cradled in his palms.

"You go check for yourself that your boyfriend's all right but don't undo those restraints until I tell you. Will you promise me that?"

"All right," she agreed finally.

"Good girl." He patted her behind. "Climb up on the bed and rest your pretty ass. I'll explain more in a second."

She walked across the room, the mirrors reflecting every angle of her body. Being naked had never been a big concern for her, but there was definitely something erotic to being so exposed considering both men were still fully dressed.

"You okay, babe?" Mark asked quietly, calmer now she was free and sitting beside him, though his fierce frown toward Sam did not abate.

As she assured him she was, she looked back at the dais. She gasped at what had been behind her. Whips, floggers and paddles had been arranged in ornate patterns on the wall behind the two posts. Cock rings, nipple clamps, ball gags, hoods and masks filled the glass-fronted cabinets on each side.

"Sam's got some…unusual tastes. That's why I thought of him when I was planning this." Mark jerked at the chains trapping him in place. "I *thought* I could trust him when I suggested it."

Sam chuckled. "Still can, ol' buddy, still can."

"Mark," she whispered. "Do you want me to let you go?"

He scrunched his eyes closed and exhaled. "You made the list—do you want to continue?"

Sam's change of plans concerned her. But having Mark at her mercy, especially after the game they'd just played with her, was intriguing. "Can we trust him?"

He frowned as Sam walked over to a cabinet and opened a door, revealing a laptop computer. There was something at the back of his eyes, like he was waging a war within himself. His hands curled into fists, his shoulder muscles tightened and a muscle in his jaw twitched before he said, "Yeah, we can trust him."

But she thought he muttered *I think* under his breath.

Well, great. He obviously wasn't comfortable with the change in plans despite his assurances.

"Now, I'll bet you're both wondering why I changed things up." Sam ignored Mark's growl. "You know we were roommates in college, right?"

Jodi nodded.

"Did he tell you how he used to watch me fucking my dates?"

She shook her head. From the corner of her eye, she saw Mark grimacing as he turned his head away from Sam. While she knew Mark loved to watch her play with herself with her vibrator, strangely the idea of Mark watching other women being fucked irritated her. So much for their little agreement not to become possessive with each other. Obviously Mark hadn't the same problem, considering he was voluntarily sharing her with Sam.

His smile fading, Sam drummed his fingers on his thigh as if he were rethinking whatever he'd had planned.

"So he'd watch you with your dates…" she prompted.

After a moment, he continued, "We worked out a system where I'd pretend to sneak them into the room, telling them he was asleep—they'd get off on the idea of having to be so quiet and not wake him up. Liked the danger of getting caught, I guess."

"But he'd really be awake the whole time, watching?"

"Sometimes he did more than just watch. Sometimes he'd join in. And then there were the times we reversed the game, and he brought his girlfriends for us to share." Sam lifted a ball gag from its hook, hefted it in his hand as he eyed Mark. "I'm thinkin' you deserve to be punished for not telling your girlfriend all this yourself."

Mark narrowed his eyes, a fierce scowl on his face. "Try it and you'll find that ball the only one you have left to play with tomorrow."

"No? No." Sam lobbed the ball gag back onto the table. "Anyway, to get to the point—"

"Too late," Mark grumbled.

"Point is," Sam continued as if he hadn't heard Mark's gibe, "since Mark didn't give you a choice about who joined you in the threesome, I reckoned that you might enjoy helping me torture your boyfriend a little. Give him a real show of the two of us enjoyin' ourselves. You know, a little turnabout being fair play and all. So are you up for my little change in plans, sweet pea?"

CHAPTER SEVEN

Something about Sam's explanation didn't quite ring true. While she didn't doubt the games they'd played in college, after all she already knew of Mark's voyeuristic tendencies, a molten undercurrent rippled between the two men. Not a macho my-dick-is-bigger-than-yours type game, but a quicksilver explosiveness from Mark, and though Sam tried to conceal it, an underlying wariness that she hadn't sensed from him at the beginning of the night.

During the game, they'd worked together with no animosity. So why had Sam felt it necessary to change the rules partway through? And was it Sam's change that had Mark glowering? Or was he simply angry at the control Sam had taken by force?

Mark definitely didn't like relinquishing control. After she'd suggested the little bondage game they'd enjoyed the week before, she'd expected that he would return the favor, let her tie him up and explore what it was like to be so completely in charge. But to her disappointment, and annoyance, he'd refused.

Is that what this was about? A "King of the Monkey bars" game between the two friends?

Men, she huffed. Fine, if he wanted to play that type of game, she'd play right along. Wouldn't hurt to take some control back from Mark after he'd manipulated this whole evening. Since he liked watching, she'd give him a show he'd never forget. With Sam's assistance, of course. She wondered if Sam could wrestle Mark up onto the dais so she could use the flogger on his ass.

When she didn't answer, Sam glanced over at her and smiled as he pocketed something. He walked toward them in an almost-predatory stalk.

"Hey, Mark, I think she likes the idea. Look at her tight little nipples, at how wide her pupils are. She's so turned on she can't even answer." He tapped Jodi on the shoulder, interrupting her fantasies. "So what's it going to be, Miz Tyler? We gonna have some more fun? Or are you gonna wimp out and call it a night? It's your decision."

His quiet question allowed the last of her concerns about Sam to float away like a feather in a breeze. He had no intention of harming her or keeping her captive. Just as Mark had originally assured her.

"Nothing's changed on my side. Mark promised me a night I'd never forget." She smiled at Mark. "And since Sam's delivered you up on a silver platter, looks like now we'll both have a memorable evening."

Jodi walked two fingers up Mark's leg, slid between his thighs and cupped his groin. When his hips jerked and his breath hissed through clenched teeth, her lips curved into a smile. "What's the matter, big guy? You enjoyed torturing me earlier with your little game. Can't handle a little return attention?"

He stared at her from beneath lowered lids, a muscle in his jaw ticking. "I can take whatever you dish out, babe."

"We'll see if you feel the same after the games I plan to play."

"You've got quite a woman here, Mark."

Another frisson of dark energy snaked between the two men before Mark shrugged in a stiff gesture. "Just so long as you back off if she tells you."

"That's a given, ol' buddy. D'you remember your safe word? It still applies, all right?" One thick brow beetled up, waiting for her answer.

Whatever aggression was bleeding from Mark, at least it wasn't directed at her. As well it shouldn't be considering he'd been tonight's architect.

"The safe word is still broccoli." She arched a cool look at Mark.

"Will you let me try a few things I noticed weren't on your list?" Sam asked.

The sight of the big man patiently waiting on her answer sent a thrill up her spine. She'd be in control of not only Mark but of him too. Except what had she forgotten to put on her list? "Yes, I trust you."

Sam rolled her nipples between his thumb and forefinger then reached into his pocket and pulled out an earring. No. Not an earring, she realized as he opened one end and clamped it over her nipple. He tugged gently, causing her pussy to clamp down and weep at the pleasure/pain it created. A moan escaped her when he attached the second clamp and tugged on them both.

Wow, nipple clamps weren't something she'd considered—they'd always looked painful. How could she have known she'd be brought nearly to orgasm by them?

"Hurt too bad?"

"No," she stammered. "It just feels…" How could pain feel so good? She must be a freak to enjoy it so much.

Seeming to understand her confusion, Sam held out his hands. "Give me your hands."

After a moment's hesitation, Jodi placed her hands in his only to find herself dragged facedown crosswise over Mark's lap once more. Sam moved away, out of her line of sight. He walked to the other side of the bed and gently stroked her pussy.

"She's so responsive, isn't she, Mark?" Sam said quietly. "You see how her hips are moving as I touch her?"

Mark's cock stirred beneath her belly, pressing into her as it thickened. Sam had been right—Mark would get off watching them fuck.

Sam made a show of licking her juices from his fingers. "Why she's as sweet as a Georgia peach."

"Enjoy it while you can, Watson," Mark sneered. "You'll never get another chance to taste her again."

A smoldering possessiveness matching the warning

in his voice made her turn her head to stare at Mark. Something dark flashed in his eyes—was he jealous? Angry? Or just incredibly turned on?

Sam patted her cheeks and walked around the bed to the other side of the room. "Stick your beautiful ass up in the air as high as you can, sweet pea. We want to make sure Mark has a good view, after all."

She adjusted her body as he'd directed, feeling a curious mix of vulnerability and excitement.

Sam typed something into the computer and grunted to himself. He scrolled the mouse and clicked a few times, then picked up a remote, aimed it at the televisions at each end of the bed. Different images appeared on the screens. The one over the bed zoomed in on Mark's face, the one at the end of the bed showed an up-close-and-personal view of her glistening labia.

Mark whistled softly.

Sam grinned. "Hey, it's the twenty-first century, ol' buddy. 4G Ultra HD LED. Only the best for this boy."

"At least it's not 3D," Jodi muttered.

Sam's grin widened. If she'd met him first, she'd have totally fallen under his spell. Which made her wonder why he didn't already have a girlfriend. Or maybe he wasn't one for monogamy. Which was more likely, she decided.

"I'm recordin' it too—I'll give you a copy when we're done."

"No way, Jose." Jodi scrambled upright, covering her breasts, only to realize the camera was now focusing on her crotch. With a foul curse, she grabbed the biggest pillow from the bed and held it in front of her. "I refuse to find this uploaded on YouTube tomorrow."

"Relax, you and Mark will have the only copy. I promise." Sam opened a cupboard beside the bed, pulled out a bag. He winked at her. "Of course if you choose to post it on the Net, I can't stop you. It won't hurt my reputation none."

Jodi shook her head. "No. No recording whatsoever. I don't like the idea of it falling into the wrong hands."

Sam's bottom lip jutted out, reminding Jodi of a child whose favorite toy had just been taken away.

Mark shared a look with Jodi, his gaze hot as he glanced at her barely covered breasts. "Can you leave the cameras on but not record?"

A smile slowly spread across Sam's face, lighting it up. "Sure can. Why don't you get back into position over Mark's lap?"

As she repositioned herself, Sam returned to the

laptop.

She squirmed as the camera slowly zoomed out, and her ass came into view. As if she didn't feel self-conscious enough about her butt; seeing it in high-definition wide-screen wasn't exactly good for the ego. Instead she concentrated on Mark, on the sweat gathering on his forehead. He wasn't watching the television at all, but her ass. She wiggled her hips to deliberately taunt him. A bead of sweat rolled down his temple, his hands flexing on the chains as if he wanted to reach out and touch her.

Sam opened a cabinet beside the bed and removed a box, placing it on the coverlet beside her. "I understand you enjoy a little anal play, Jodi. Or was Mark shinin' me on?"

Jodi turned her head to stare at the bulge in Sam's pants. The muscles in her ass clenched at the thought of being penetrated by the thick cock outlined in black leather. "Um, I like it when *he* does it."

A grin split Sam's face when he saw where Jodi was looking. He cupped his bulging groin. "You worrying that ol' Sam Junior here's not gonna fit into that tight little ass of yours? Well now, you don't worry 'bout a thing, 'cause I'm gonna prepare you so it won't hurt."

"Go slow, Sam, she's real tight," Mark warned, which made her ass tighten even more.

Moments later, the bed dipped beneath Sam's weight. Huge gel-covered fingers came into the camera's view, briefly hovered over her ass. They separated her cheeks, spread the cool gel around her entrance. One finger penetrated her knuckle-deep, pressed farther, spreading the gel deep inside of her. Watching what Sam was doing on the wide screen, and feeling it at the same time was a strange sensation but knowing Mark was watching another man touching her ass was a turn-on she'd never expected.

Her eyes widened when a bright red butt plug came into view, pressed against her opening. That sucker was huge, way bigger than any man's cock she'd ever seen. And definitely bigger than the plug Mark had bought for her when they'd first tried anal sex.

"It's too big." Her breath caught in her throat. She tried to move away but his hands held her firmly in place.

"It's just the camera—remember they say it adds ten pounds?" Sam chuckled.

He leaned over, his leather pants cool against the back of her thighs as he whispered into her ear, "Trust me. I know how much Mark loves watching me fucking a woman's ass."

Mark groaned. "Way to remind Jodi of my past lovers, Watson."

Sam caressed her neck, then moved lower, easing the tension that had crept into her shoulders. But for all his efforts, Jodi tensed when the tip of the plug intruded.

"Just take nice slow, deep breaths, and think how much fun it's going to be tormenting old Mark over there."

"You don't have to do this, Jodi," Mark rasped. "You can still tell him to stop."

"I'm okay." Her ass burning, she scrunched her eyes closed as the plug penetrated the first tight ring.

"Just relax, Jodi. Remember to breathe." Sam pressed the plug deeper in a relentless motion. "I'm not hurting you now, am I, sweet pea?"

Jodi shook her head. "No, it just feels weird knowing it's not Mark touching me there."

And hot. So hot. Her pussy ached to be filled too.

"Open your eyes. Watch how hot Mark's getting. See how he's straining against those restraints?"

Mark's lips were white as he captured them between his teeth, the veins in his biceps stood out in stark relief as his grip on the chains tightened.

Sam whispered, his free hand stroking her ass in a gentle caress. "He's like a dog ready to attack. To protect you. Or to take you for his own."

With a smooth movement, Sam pushed the butt plug up as far as it would go, then pulled her from Mark's lap until she was draped over his arm like a femme fatale in a thirties movie. A sizzling jolt shot up her spine when he tugged on the nipple clamp with his teeth. With a final tug, he lay her down beside Mark and returned to the laptop.

"Spread your legs real wide for me. You can lean against Mark if you want but face out so I can taste your sweet honey some more."

Squirming until she was cradled between Mark's arm and body, she arranged her legs at the side of bed and rested her head on Mark's chest. Despite the size of the plug that stretched her ass, she was surprisingly comfortable. Though it was definitely larger than the one she had at home, this plug really wasn't as big as it had looked. It must have been the camera accentuating the size, she decided.

The images on the television changed to two of her from different angles, one zoomed in close to her groin, the other showing her full body from above the bed. Sam crawled onto the bed and lifted one of her legs over his shoulder. With a bright grin, he glanced up at her. "I've been looking forward to this all night."

He lowered his head. Fascinated, Jodi watched on the big screen as he ran his tongue up her labia, the warmth swirling in intricate patterns, never quite touching her clitoris. The carnal intrusion shot bolts of energy to every nerve ending, starting a smoldering fire that quickly burst into a conflagration when his tongue finally touched her core.

She grabbed at the silk comforter on either side of her hips, gasping, arching her hips. A broad hand lay flat across her belly, holding her in place.

"Don't make me tie you down too." His words rippled against her sensitized flesh, rumbled through her bones and set off another firestorm.

"Jodi? Open your eyes. Look at Mark."

When had she closed them? Her lids heavy, she turned her head and saw sweat running down Mark's brow, his fingers alternately opening then closing around the chains.

"Oh, baby, I wish that was me going down on you." His voice sounded rough, like he'd been singed by the flames she was sure were shooting from her.

Sam drew back for a moment and dragged a finger over her labia, dipped it into her pussy. He smeared her cream across her mouth then dipped his head again, thrusting his tongue into her pussy.

"Let me lick it off you, baby," Mark whispered. "Let me taste what Sam's tasting."

Arching her back, Jodi captured Mark's mouth with her own, tasting the salty sweat on his upper lip. He thrust his tongue into her mouth, mimicking Sam's motions.

In desperation, her hands sought Mark's erection. Sam grabbed her hands and pushed them firmly by her side.

"Oh, no, none of that. He just gets to watch this time."

Sam resumed his attentions, one hand tugging on a nipple clamp, sending a bolt of heat straight to her pussy, and her blood boiling through her veins. He slipped one finger inside her, then another. When he pressed on the butt plug while this tongue flicked just the right place, she shattered.

With an easy movement, Sam tugged his shirt off. Her eyes widened to see a long, ugly scar marring his chest, but then he undid his fly, letting his leathers fall to the floor. His scar forgotten, Jodi sucked in a breath at the sight of his cock, and knew he hadn't misjudged the need for such a big butt plug.

He hopped onto the bed and arranged the pillows beside Mark, ensuring he didn't come close to Mark's hand, and lay down.

"Crawl on up here. Let me feel that soft mouth of yours on Sam Junior."

She stifled her snort. There was nothing *junior* about that thick pole. He slid his hand along its length and back down, squeezing the tip on each pass, a bead of pearly moisture glistening at its tip.

"Don't take your eyes off Mark." As she caught Mark's gaze, she saw the hunger deep in his eyes. The lust. And something deeper, almost feral.

"Start off licking my balls," Sam commanded. His hand lifted them as his hips thrust closer to her.

With each swipe of her tongue, Mark's breathing got heavier, his eyes half closing.

"Now lick my cock. Make a meal of me."

She began with a teasing nip to the base of his shaft, then swirled her tongue up the thick shaft, tracing the dark veins that bulged from the taut skin. Her eyes still on Mark, she made a show of spreading the drop of come that quivered at the end of *Junior's* slit over her lips. Then delicately, slowly, licked it off.

Feeling power spread through her at having such a captive audience, Jodi opened her mouth, tightened her lips over Junior's head and swallowed him deep.

"Watch her, Mark. Look at how her lips are stretching over my shaft. Oh shit, that feels so good!" Sam threw his head back and arched his hips as she increased the suction. The noise of her sucking and Mark's harsh pants mingled with Sam's murmured instructions.

Jodi tasted a trickle of pre-come on the back of her tongue, slightly more acidic than Mark's essence. Her hand drifted down between her legs, thrust inside in a feeble attempt to mimic the motions of her mouth, her tongue. Cream coated her fingers, slid down her thighs as her hips thrust. She rolled her clit between her thumb and forefinger, moaning as the pressure inside her built like a volcano about to explode.

Fingers wrapped in her hair forcing her to resume the movement she'd forgotten while pleasuring herself. Eventually he held her head still, his hips pistoning his cock deep into her mouth.

"She's giving me the best blow job I've ever had,

Mark. But you know that, don't you? I'll bet you're wishing…her lips were…around your cock, aren't you?" Sam said, his voice deepening with every thrust. "Isn't her ass beautiful? Can you imagine me…parting those sweet cheeks of hers…taking her ass?"

CHAPTER EIGHT

S am's taunts caused Mark's guts to cramp like he'd swallowed a length of razor wire.

What had he been thinking, suggesting a threesome with Sam? Why had he thought he'd be okay sharing Jodi with any man, let alone a player like Sam?

Jodi moaned, her hand moving frantically between her arching hips as Sam thrust his dick down her throat. Mark wanted to plant a fist in Sam's face when he saw his friend's eyes scrunched closed, a look of ecstasy on his face. Ecstasy from Jodi sucking him off. They'd discussed a similar scenario, but he was supposed to be satisfying Jodi from behind while she went down on Sam. And he'd never thought about what it would feel like, how his heart would tear watching Sam enjoying Jodi's attentions. It had never mattered before with any of their girlfriends in college.

Why had Sam changed up their plan? Despite what Sam had told Jodi, he knew his friend had some hidden reason for tying him to the bed and forcing him to watch the two of them fucking. But what?

Jodi's cheeks hollowed and her neck worked as she swallowed. Sam's groan made Mark's cock ache as it remembered what it felt like to be deep-throated by Jodi. To have that wonderful tongue of hers caress every millimeter of sensitive skin. The amazing suction she had, coaxing every last drop of come from his balls.

He shifted his hips, attempting to relieve the pain in his cock, not only from being trapped beneath too-tight denim, but from its need to bury itself in her, to feel those tight muscles grasp him, contract around him as she found her release. Yet here he was—a spectator.

For what felt like the fiftieth time that night, Mark grasped the chains binding him to the bed and tugged in a futile effort to free himself. He had to stop this travesty. He had to snatch Jodi away from Sam and finish within her. Hear her scream her release. A release only he could bring her.

Then he'd take Sam down—crush his balls, cut off his dick—whatever it took to punish him for daring to take Jodi in front of him like this. And yell at Jodi for agreeing to Sam's suggestion.

His head fell back on the pillow, his conscience mocking him with a taunting laugh. Hell, who was he kidding? He'd been the one who had suggested, no, forced Jodi to write that damned list of fantasies. He'd been the one who had initially suggested the whole idea to Sam, not the other way around. He'd been the one to talk Jodi into the whole idea upstairs. And now he was the one trapped in a nightmare caused by his own hubris. Forced to watch his lover bringing his best friend to the height of ecstasy.

Another deep-throated moan escaped Jodi's lips. Mark closed his eyes as his cock pulsed, remembering the feel of those moans the last time she'd gone down on him. His spine tingled and his hips arched, seeking relief. Seeking Jodi.

If he could just get free…

"Sam, at least release one hand so I can jerk off. This is fucking torture to watch."

Without changing the rhythm of his hips, Sam opened his eyes. Shot a dark look of warning as he shook his head.

Goddamn it, what was that bastard playing at? It was like Sam expected him to know something. Understand something. But what?

Then all of a sudden Sam pulled his cock from Jodi's mouth. "Not yet."

A camera whirred overhead, the image on the screens capturing the moisture on Sam's still-erect cock. Caught a thin stream of come leaking from the slit and trickling down the head onto Jodi's mouth. Another camera zoomed in on Jodi's beautiful pink tongue as it skimmed over her bottom lip, and lingered on a glistening drop of Sam's come.

The barbed wire in his guts heated, snaked around his balls and tightened.

It should be his come she tasted. *His.*

What had possessed him to think he could sit idly by watching Jodi get off with another man, that he could share her? No man was ever going to touch her again. Only him. Jodi was his and his alone. And he was hers. Forever.

Whoa, where had that come from?

How many times had he and Sam shared their girl-friends back in college? Yet never before had he felt the icy-hot poker of jealousy now stabbing his gut. What was it about Jodi that caused him to feel like a guard dog protecting his property? His private property.

You're trying to pretend she's like all those other women you and Sam shared, his conscience mocked. But she's not. You've fallen in love with her.

"On your hands and knees, sugar."

If he'd been standing, he would have had to sit down and put his head between his knees. Holy shit, he loved her. Head-over-heels, deep-down-in-the-gut, 'til-death-do-us-part in love with her.

And stupid ass that he was, he'd voluntarily shared her with another man. He'd even encouraged her, told her it was okay to fuck someone else. And she'd agreed.

What if that meant… He swallowed hard, the barbed wire tightening until his balls felt like they were about to drop off. What if she didn't love him? What if when this was over, she wanted to have more three-somes, to force him to watch her fuck other men? Or worse, what if she stopped inviting him to join in?

Shit! What had he done?

A cold worm crawled through his intestines. A worm wearing razor-sharp spikes that ripped his guts apart as he remembered their agreement. After the first time they'd made love, he'd insisted there be no long-term attachments. That either one of them could walk away any time. And she'd agreed. Except, when he should have been clearing the mountains of paperwork he faced every day, he'd found himself fantasizing about fucking her on the desk, on the floor, against the wall. No, he amended, not fucking her, loving her.

"See okay there, buddy?"

Pulled from considering the ramifications of this revelation, Mark glanced over at Sam. Who smirked.

Is that what this was about? Did Sam realize that he loved Jodi before even he did? Was he trying to force Mark to get jealous? To acknowledge that Jodi was his and his alone? Knowing Sam, he'd never live that down.

"Ol' buddy?" Sam asked again, tilting his head toward the big screens. "You see okay?"

There in living Technicolor, larger than life, Jodi's ass filled the screen. The bright red butt plug a perfect target for Sam's goddamned cock.

His already-erect cock jerked as if trying to punch through the fly. Say no! it screamed. Stop this.

Sweat dripped down Mark's temples and his arms shook as they strained against the restraints. His mouth opened, wanting to tell them to stop. But the words stuck in his throat, tangled in the wire that ensnared his whole body.

What if she doesn't love me? How pathetic would that be?

JODI STARED AT THE FLAT-SCREEN IMAGE as Sam's condom-covered cock bobbed into view. Watched it slide across her glistening swollen folds, watched as it buried itself into the dark pink opening stretching her drum-tight. Between the pressure of the plug up her ass and him stretching her pussy, she could feel every beat of his heart in the head of his cock.

A slow exhalation was followed by a moan as he began the gentle push and pull, exciting every inch of her, inside and out. "It's like a fucking velvet glove's wrapped around my dick."

Sam's fingers tightened on her hips as he began to rock into her, his movement quickly changing to a pounding rhythm. He reached around her front, one hand giving a nipple clamp a wicked tug, a movement that streaked to her core. The nipple clamps brushed the bulge in Mark's jean with each thrust of Sam's hips.

Mark's hips pumped as if he were fucking her too.

Imagining freeing his cock, sucking it while Sam plowed into her drove her up to the edge of the abyss and pushed her over. Her hips bucked as her orgasm ripped through her in a wildfire of sensation.

"Not—done—yet." Sam groaned.

He slammed into her, burying himself to his balls, each time his stomach pressed against the butt plug, moving it just enough to drive her wild. If it was possible his cock thickened and pushed even deeper, stretching her until she thought she would burst.

When he stiffened and shouted, his hot stream of come pulsing hard inside her set off yet another firestorm. She shuddered through her orgasm, unable to gather breath enough to moan.

Sam caught her just before she collapsed onto Mark's lap, eased his cock from her body. "Damn, woman, I didn't want to come that soon."

"Come on, Sam. Let me free. I've got the mother of all hard-ons—my dick's hurtin' real bad here." Mark spoke through gritted teeth. Jodi opened her eyes and saw flames in the back of Mark's eyes, flames of lust, flames of fury.

A trickle of fear grew in her belly, tightening her

diaphragm and driving the breath from her.

Had she made a mistake agreeing to Sam's plan? Mark was the one who had arranged this. *Hadn't that been what he'd wanted all along?* Shit, had she blown their relationship? Did he see her now only as a whore? Or was that what he thought of her in the first place to suggest this whole scenario? Could she convince him she wanted him more than anyone else?

Sam gestured with his head toward Mark. "Unzip loverboy's jeans. But nothing more."

Seeing heat flash in Mark's eyes, she fumbled with his zipper. Yeah, she'd blown it. And the man she loved now despised her.

"Undo the restraints, Jodi," Mark ordered quietly so Sam couldn't hear.

If she let him go now, would he walk away? Not only from the bed and the room but from her?

She licked her top lip when she saw his engorged cock outlined by the dark denim. A glance over her shoulder showed a bare-assed Sam fiddling with his computer, not paying any attention to what she was doing.

Her hands snaked around Mark's hips, and drew his jeans down to his knees. His underwear quickly followed suit. She shoved her hands under his ass and grabbed his buttocks while she licked the taut, satiny head. In a violent motion his hips arched up, shoved his cock through her lips until it touched her throat. God, he tasted so good! This felt so right. Wildly desperate, her nails dug into his ass, her mouth sucking, needing to make him come deep in her throat, needing to taste him.

The mattress dipped behind her. Fingers parted her labia and started playing with her clit. They moved expertly, pressing against her most sensitive areas, driving her wild with need. When two fingers penetrated her and stroked deep inside, she struggled to match the rhythm she knew Mark loved, needed.

Please don't pull me away, she silently pleaded to Sam.

Except Sam didn't hear her silent entreaty. Instead he withdrew his fingers and grasped her hips. Stopped her motion. Mark cursed volubly when Sam pulled her away.

"No," she moaned. "Please, Sam, I want to do this for Mark. I need him."

Sam leaned over her shoulder and whispered in her ear. "Then ride him, sweet pea."

Before Sam could retract his suggestion, Jodi swung her leg over Mark and sheathed him in one movement. She braced herself on his shoulders and rotated her hips, grinding his cock deep against her womb. All memory of Sam lost, she merged herself with Mark, their bodies moving in a sinuous dance. Just as she was climbing the final peak, she felt a hand on her shoulder, pressing her toward Mark.

"Let him suck those luscious tits," Sam instructed.

"How am I supposed to suck them with these on?" Mark snagged one leather tassel in his teeth and growled. The pressure from the clamp pulled on her nipple, sending a bolt of lightning into her core.

Chuckling, Sam removed the nipple clamps and dropped them on the bed beside her. Mark laved the tender peaks. The soothing gesture was at odds to the fierce expression in his eyes; the soft words he murmured defied the bunched muscles in his arms and shoulders that threatened violence.

Sam said something but her mind was in such a whirl from Mark's attentions that she didn't hear. This—this was what she wanted. The two of them so close together she'd lost track of where she stopped and he began.

She was pulled from the brink when Sam pulled the butt plug out in a smooth movement.

His broad hand pressed against the back of her neck, laying her flat over Mark. "Don't worry. You keep on lovin' your man there. I'm just fixin' to perform item number seven on your list."

Her mind whirled, her thoughts a morass. What was item seven?

Oh shit! She'd said she wanted to have two men inside her at the same time. Did she want that? Should she tell him no? She buried her head in the crook of Mark's neck. What would it be like to feel another cock warming her, caressing her in both places at the same time? Of course she wanted to try this. Look how empty she'd felt when he'd removed the butt plug. And she might never get another chance. She consciously relaxed against Mark and murmured, "All right."

Thick fingers smeared cool gel over her ass and she felt that broad head nudge her tender opening. In a smooth movement, he pushed the head of his cock past the tight ring of her anus.

"Shit, Mark, she's so fuckin' tight." Sam groaned as he thrust into her deeper.

In an unconscious protest, she whimpered as Sam

continued his relentless assault.

"Sam, stop, you're hurting her." Mark wrapped his hands on the chains holding him in place and pulled them tight. "Goddamn it, stop!"

"No, don't stop. Please," Jodi gasped. "Mark, he's not hurting me."

Sam curled over her, his wiry chest hair tickling her back. "Relax, sweet pea, breathe."

Her whimper changed to a deep-throated moan as the hot pain of her ass combined with the white flare of pleasure in her pussy. Arching her back, she pushed against his shaft. Mark shifted inside her, the pressure of being stretched by the two cocks an erotic assault that sent fireballs rocketing through her system.

"Oh yeah, that's what I'm talkin' about." The slow glide stopped as he seated himself deep inside. He tenderly stroked her back as he waited for her to adjust.

He rocked into her in languid thrusts, pushing and pulling her cheeks apart as his cock stroked the walls of her ass.

Mark tilted his hips and began to match his movements to Sam's, never taking his gaze from Jodi's face.

"*Eres mia.*" Mark's eyes flashed and though whatever he'd said sounded beautiful, it wasn't said with his usual fluid grace. If anything, he ground out the words as a statement, a declaration. A challenge.

"*Eres mia, solo mia,*" he said again as he thrust deep within her.

"Do you know what he's saying?" Sam asked quietly.

Jodi shook her head.

He leaned closer, whispering so only she could hear. "He's saying '*you're mine, only mine.*'"

Tears filled her eyes at the translation. Did she dare hope that he loved her too?

"I'm yours, only yours," she whispered, pressing her lips against his.

"*Te amo.*" He captured her lips, joined them until they were both panting for breath. "*Te amo,* Jodi. *Te amo.*"

That one needed no translation. "I love you too."

The sweetness of Mark's declaration combined with the sensation of being so exquisitely filled, sandwiched between the two men, set her senses into overload. The fireworks sparkling at the edge of her vision exploded, a comet flaring across the sky. She came down from the heavens to hear Sam's deep groan as he filled her with liquid heat.

She collapsed against Mark's chest, her arms and legs shaking, unable to move. Sam withdrew and rolled to the side.

Before she'd regained her strength, a large hand slapped her tender behind.

"You're a very bad girl, Jodi," Sam said. "I only gave you permission to unzip Mark's fly, not blow him. And you definitely weren't supposed to fuck him yet."

But despite his stern manner, a broad grin lit his face. He leaned over and pressed a kiss on her cheek. "Thank you, sweet pea. Now, you'd better undo loverboy there before he starts to incinerate."

A promise in her smile, Jodi scrambled around and undid the restraint binding Mark's left ankle, then his right.

She lingered before undoing the arm restraints, teased his nipples, dipped one finger into his navel, curled her fingers around his cock and stroked the still-engorged head. Had he not completed when she and Sam had?

"Undo the damned wrist straps, will you?" he growled.

The moment she'd loosened the final clasp, Mark flipped Jodi onto the bed and held her in place with the weight of his body. Entered her. Claimed her.

CHAPTER NINE

Mark ploughed his cock into Jodi as if possessed, desperate to claim her back as his own, desperate to make her body forget what it felt like to have another man's cock stretching her, filling her.

"You're mine! *Only* mine," he growled.

When she wrapped her legs around his waist, welcoming him, his groans battled with the squeaks of the bed and the slap of his thighs against hers.

Embers burst into flame, rocketing down his spine. His balls tightened against his body, but he kept ramming into her until she screamed her release, something she hadn't done with Sam he noted with masculine pride.

Now. *Now.* His essence erupted, molten lava into a white-hot cavern, an explosion of love and anger and jealousy.

He collapsed on top of her, laying there for a few minutes, his breathing rough. Resting his forehead against hers, he stroked her face, crooning to her in Spanish knowing she wouldn't understand, and his tone gentle so she wouldn't know he cursed Sam, cursed himself. His touch trailed down her neck, stroked her shoulders, while his head dipped to kiss the reddened flesh of her breasts.

"*Te amo,*" he whispered. Had he said that earlier? He'd been thinking it. And had she said she loved him too? Not wanting to take the chance that she might not have understood, he repeated it in English. "I love you, Jodi."

"I love you too," she whispered.

He closed his eyes and said a silent prayer of thanks, and a vow that he'd never again allow another man to touch her the way Sam had. The way he'd invited Sam to.

Desperate to remove any trace of the other man from her skin, Mark touched everywhere Sam had touched. Everywhere Sam had tasted, Mark tasted. The memory of watching Sam's fingers on her soft flesh, of his cock stretching her pussy, and knowing he'd been the one to suggest it would be something he'd never forgive himself for.

Jodi tried to lift her hips but failed to move him. No way was he going to let her go until he'd made things right between them.

A flicker of pain crossed her face and she squirmed beneath him again.

"Aw, baby, did I hurt you?" He lifted his weight from her, but kept his arms stabbed into the mattress on either side of her, trapping her.

Her eyes fluttered open, a dazed and exhausted look filling them. "I think I'm lying on the nipple clamps."

Damn things. Mark reached beneath her. With a flick of his wrist, he withdrew the offending clamps and tossed them across the floor.

Mark rolled over and pulled her beside him, wrapping his arms around her in an iron grip. "Sam, this is en—"

He trailed off when he realized they were alone in the room, Sam nowhere in sight. Another stream of curses directed at both Sam and himself echoed off the walls.

"Mark?" Jodi said quietly, her eyes veiled as she glanced down at his chest. "Did you want me to tell Sam no when he asked? Did I screw things up between us?"

He cursed himself again, softer this time, when he realized she thought he would blame her, that he might be angry that she'd agreed to Sam's suggestion. "I know it was my idea originally, but I couldn't…"

He averted his gaze, glancing at the mountain of pillows surrounding them. "When Sam and I discussed tonight's…entertainment…I thought I'd have no problem watching you with Sam. You know how I love to watch you play with yourself. And he wasn't lying about what we used to do back in college."

He took a deep breath and forced himself to look at her. Damn it, she still wasn't looking at him. Was she angry with him? Or had she found more pleasure with Sam?

"When it came down to it, to actually sharing you…" Words that usually flowed easily for him lodged in his chest. What if she thought about what he'd asked of her? What if she realized how he'd violated her trust by failing to protect her? "When Sam talked about penetrating your ass, when he touched you, this wave of anger started burning in my gut."

No shit, he'd felt like a caveman who wanted to grab her by the hair and carry her back to his cave. To beat Sam until his best friend lay bloodied and unmoving at his feet.

Her eyes squeezed shut as she turned her head away from him. "You *are* angry that I agreed."

He could have lost her tonight. He could still lose her.

He stroked the side of her face until her eyes opened and she slowly turned her head back to look at him. "No, babe. I'm not angry that you agreed. I could never be angry about that. It was my stupid idea, remember?"

"Not stupid," she said softly.

"I'm sorry. I'm so sorry for tonight and what I put you through."

She pushed away from him, shaking her head. "Sorry? For what? Because I have to tell you, I'm not."

"I behaved like a jerk. I should have asked you if you really wanted a threesome. I should have asked if there was anyone you wanted more. I should never have pressured you. I should… I…" His Adam's apple jerked as he swallowed, remembering the anger that had engulfed him when Sam had tied him to the bed, when he'd been forced to watch. "I was insane thinking I could share you."

"Ssshhh." She pressed a finger to his lips, silencing him. Her touch was soothing, as if she could sense his fear, his feelings of inadequacy. "You did give me a choice, remember? So did Sam. It's not like he hurt me or anything. We had a safe word—I could have used it any time."

He didn't want to remind her that a safe word was only good if the other person backed off. But Sam would have stopped—or he never would have trusted the bastard in the first place. Some of his anger bled away. And he had the rest of his life to make it up to her. For now, it was enough she forgave him.

For someone who had seen the worst life could throw at a person, she was so forgiving, so open. He was going to buy her the biggest diamond ring he could find. A diamond that would tell every other guy in the world "hands off, she's mine!"

If she'd wear it.

CHAPTER TEN

His stomach grumbling, Mark eased his arm from under Jodi and pulled the silk sheet over her. She squirmed, tugging her pillow closer beneath her but stayed asleep.

He picked up the remote Sam had used earlier and turned off the big screens one by one. Finding his blue jeans was more of a challenge—he ended up unearthing them from under the comforter they'd kicked off the bed. And his underwear was nowhere to be seen. Hell, he'd just go commando.

"Be right back, babe." A soft mewl escaped Jodi's lips when he bent down to brush a kiss across her forehead.

Barefoot, he padded from the room and climbed the stairs to the main level. A green-tinged light spilled from the office into the hallway. The creak of the leather chair, and a snap and hiss of a can opening told him where Sam had disappeared.

Time to settle that account.

His feet on the desk, ankles crossed, Sam leaned back in the chair, staring at the flat-screen television on the far wall, a Heineken in his hand. His leather pants had been traded in for a pair of grey fleece track pants, and, like Mark, he wore no shirt.

Muttering, Sam lifted the glass in a salute to the screen. The screen with an image of Jodi sleeping.

Mark cursed under his breath. Sam had been watching them this whole time?

With a snort of disgust, Mark walked into the room and flicked off the television. "And you accused me of being a voyeur."

Sam scratched idly at the scar on his chest. "Considering the glass house you live in, you shouldn't be tossing stones at me. 'Sides, I didn't have the sound turned up."

As if that made a difference.

Mark stared down at his friend. "Do you want to tell

me why the fuck you thought it necessary to tie me up, *ol' buddy*?"

Sam placed the can on the desk, turned it until a dark circle of moisture imprinted on the blotter. Lifted it and placed it beside where it had been. Turned it again, making another circle.

"I did what I had to," he said.

Mark folded his arms across his chest. "You want to explain that?"

Another circle joined the others on the blotter. Then a fifth and a sixth. Sam finally lifted his gaze and met Mark's. "I didn't want to see you toss away a sure thing playing the games we played in college. You're not cut out for that lifestyle, Mark. And from what I've seen of her, neither's Jodi."

"If you thought it was wrong, you could have walked away. You could have not agreed in the first place."

Sam met his gaze evenly. "You said if I didn't help you, you'd find someone else. Couldn't take that chance."

"So you took control by tying me up."

Sam lifted the glass halfway to his lips then stopped. "Only way I could think of to prove my point."

"That having a ménage is a college game? Just how did tying me up prove that?"

"My *point* was that you love that woman." Sam stabbed his hand through the air toward the television. "And she loves you. Didn't you see how she was looking at you when she asked you if she should continue? Shit, man, it was soul-deep love. Jodi's a one-man woman. She deserves a one-woman man. Someone who'll protect her. Love her. Who won't share her with anyone else. She's too damn special to have you offer her around to your friends so you can get off."

Mark snorted, but his anger evaporated as fast as a water drop on a hot griddle. He slumped into the chair on the opposite side of the desk. "You're right. I do love her. But I didn't realize that until tonight. What tipped you off?"

"Every time you said her name you got this goofy look on your face." Sam took another sip of his drink, then held up the can and glared at it, frowning. "But you were so damned determined to bring me in as your third, kept telling me it was just like 'the old days'. That you two were just partners having a little fun. You were trying too hard to convince yourself, ya know?

"And then tonight…when I touched her…I've

never seen that look on your face before. You looked like you were ready to tear my head off."

"I was," Mark conceded.

"Yet you let me continue. Let her think you were cool with sharing her. And that was flat-out wrong." Sam set the can down and gave Mark a hard stare. "So I figured I had to do something to get through that thick skull of yours. Make you realize how good you got it."

Mark ran a hand over his scalp. "Yet this conscience of yours didn't stop you from fucking her, did it? You want to explain that one?"

One of Sam's shoulders pulled up in a halfhearted shrug. "It was all her choice. She could have used the safe word at any time. And don't forget that when I put the proposition to her, she asked you and you said—"

"I told her she could trust you. I let it go on." Mark scrubbed at his face, then dropped his hands into his lap. "I get your point. No more ménages. I don't think I could hold myself back if another man touched her. I'd probably rip his head off."

Sam closed his eyes and exhaled noisily. "Thank the good Lord above for that! She's a special lady." Sam leaned forward, planted his elbows on the desk. He pointed at Mark as if his fingers were a gun. "But you hear me, Mark, and you remember me well. If you mistreat her, if you fuck around on her, I'm gonna be on your ass like a hound dog on a hare. We straight?"

"You'd have to get in line," Jodie said from the doorway.

"Thanks for the offer, Sam, but if Mark ever fools around on me, I can take care of him myself." Jodi scissored her fingers together. "And I'll be more brutal than Lorena Bobbitt. If he fools around on me, Mark won't have any balls to tuck into his jockeys by the time I'm done with him."

Both men immediately crossed their legs.

Sam barked a laugh and pounded his fist on the desk so hard the phone jumped out of its base. "I think you've finally found someone who can keep you in line, ol' buddy."

"I wouldn't have it any other way." Mark grinned back. "Come over here, *Lorena.*"

JODI SAUNTERED OVER TO MARK, conscious of the hungry look in his eyes as he tracked her. She bent to kiss him but stopped an inch away from his lips, murmuring, "Oh, and by the way, if you think I'm going to invite another woman to our bed as a quid pro quo for tonight, I should warn you. It ain't gonna happen."

"I don't want anyone else." Mark pulled her onto his lap and nuzzled her neck.

"Man, if you two are going to get all mushy on me, I'm leavin'," Sam drawled then drained the remainder of his drink.

Jodi pulled away. "Don't leave, Sam. I want to thank you for what you did tonight." Color rose up her neck. "I mean, about tying Mark up—that *was* to make him jealous, wasn't it?"

He glanced away, as if unwilling to meet her gaze. "Yeah, well…"

"I appreciate what you did—especially since it could have backfired on you." She leaned over and kissed his cheek, then cocked her head and looked at him. "You know, I've got a friend I think you might like…"

He held up both his hands in mock surrender. "No thank you. I'm not desperate enough for a blind date." He grew serious as he glanced between them. "Look, if later on, down the road, you two decide you want a third in bed again, you call me, all right? And, Jodi, don't let Mark here ever force you to do something you don't want to do. He does, you call me and I'll pound some sense into his head."

"Thanks." She laughed and patted his hand. "You're a good friend, Sam."

"Man, how'd that sonuvabitch get so lucky in snatching you up?" He hung his head and shook it. When he lifted it, a sly smile crept over his broad face, lighting a twinkle in his eyes. "You sure you wouldn't consider coming to work for me back east? I'm always on the lookout for a good security consultant."

Jodi laughed and looped her arms around Mark's neck. "Nah, not a chance." She sobered. Sam's request reminded her of something that had been bugging her all night. "You know, Sam, I've been wondering…"

"Why am I thinkin' I should be worried?" Sam quirked an eyebrow.

"I've been wondering why you left the combination to the safe where I could find it. You did that deliberately, didn't you? Were you testing my competence? Do you think I'm not good enough for your company?"

Mark swore under his breath. "No wonder you took that bet that you could crack it in under two minutes. You had the combination the whole time, you cheater."

"You know I never bet unless I'm absolutely sure I

can win." She turned back to Sam. "I could have cracked the safe without the combination, you know."

Sam shrugged one shoulder. "Yeah, I know."

"So why make it easy on me? Why leave the combination where anyone could find it?"

The shoulder hitched up again. He crushed the can and tossed it in the trash. "You might not have found it."

She paused, watched him deliberately avoid her gaze. "There's something more here, isn't there?"

When he didn't answer, Mark straightened. "Sam? What are you hiding?"

Sam turned the chair sideways, eyed the door. "It's no biggie. Just forget about it, okay?" He opened the door to a small fridge built into the credenza. "Y'all want a drink? I've got ginger ale, beer, you name it."

"Sam?" Mark persisted.

"Oh, all right." Sam picked up another beer can then exchanged it for a bottle of Pellegrini. "It was part of a bet. Satisfied?"

Jodi turned to Mark and raised one brow in query. "Don't look at me, babe."

When both sets of eyes turned on him, Sam continued, "I told my assistant to let you in without the usual security check so you'd buy into Mark's story about the place needing an upgrade in its security. But that woman was like a starving dog with a T-bone and wouldn't let it go until I explained exactly why I wanted to let you in."

Heat crept up Jodi's neck as she thought of the straitlaced assistant and what she might think if she knew what had really gone on that evening. She pressed her fingers to her mouth. "Please tell me you didn't tell her what you really had planned for tonight."

Sam scowled. "I do have some discretion, you know. I told her I was checking out the efficiency of Mark's employees as part of the merger agreement. Told her I'd challenged him to have you break into the safe."

"But that doesn't explain why you left the combination for me to find."

Sam eyed the door again, reminding her of how she'd felt trapped earlier that evening.

"Well, you see, I figured being a former cop and everything, you weren't a real girly girl." He slid down in his chair, his chin on his chest, then grasped the handles of his chair, until it groaned in protest. His next words came out in a rush. "I figured you wouldn't really clean things the way a maid would. Figured that you'd sort of dust around things, you know. But Sandy…Ms. Hallquist, she said if you were as good as Mark claimed, you'd be…" He shifted his weight again.

"That I'd be what?" Jodi asked, trying to hide the laughter caused by seeing the big man squirm in discomfort.

"That you'd be…you know…snoopy." The words left him in a rush.

"Snoopy?" Jodi laughed aloud. "Sam, I was reconnoitering for security flaws. Of course, I'd be snoopy!"

Obviously relieved that she wasn't offended, Sam let his shoulders drop and leaned back in his chair. "Sandy bet me that if she wrote the combination on the blotter—"

"—I'd find it." Jodi finished for him. "Which I wouldn't have unless I cleared the desk when I dusted."

"How much d'you lose?" Mark asked. Jodi could feel his muscles rippling as he tried not to laugh aloud.

Sam's cheeks turned bright red as he mumbled, "I have to enter myself in the annual bachelor auction to raise money for the homeless women's shelter."

Mark's laughter exploded, nearly unseating Jodi. "Oh, that's fucking perfect! Jodi, we have to go to that auction. I want to watch him squirm while all those women ogle his ass."

Sam looked up, a look of hope flickering in his eyes. "Hey, Jodi, maybe you could bid on me. You know, save a poor helpless bachelor from those biddies?"

Mark shook his head. "Not a chance! You made the bet, you suffer the consequences."

"I don't…" Jodi started, then hesitated as a thought struck her. But would her plan work, especially with the two huge egos these men had? "Maybe we could come to some arrangement."

"Jodi," Mark groaned. "Don't you dare buy into his 'poor bachelor' crap. I want to watch him strut his sorry ass down a runway like a frickin' supermodel—it's the perfect payback, babe."

Jodi bit her bottom lip. "I'll make the highest bid on you if you promise me something."

"What's that?" Sam eyed her as if she were a python ready to strike.

She pushed herself off Mark's lap, paced as she figured out exactly how to word her request so as not to offend either man. Finally she stopped and took a deep breath. "It's about the merger. Mark loves Celada Security. He's worked real hard to get it where it is, and I'm afraid that when you take over—"

"Jodi," Mark said quietly. "Sam and I are good. You don't need to worry—"

Sam held up a hand, stopping Mark. "Let her have her say, Mark. She's just looking out for your interests. And I respect the hell out of her for that."

"If things don't work out," she continued, not wanting to meet Mark's eyes, "the two companies revert back to the way things are now. And you'll guarantee Hauberk won't compete for any contracts against Celada in Texas."

Sam opened a drawer and pulled out a thick folder, tossed it on the desk. "If it sets your mind at ease, Mark and I already had something similar written into the contract. Here's my copy—you can see for yourself."

Mark rested his hand over hers, his thumb gently stroking her wrist. "Considering he's the buying company, Sam didn't have to have that written in, babe. But he's the one who suggested it even before we put anything on paper."

Sam shrugged and glanced away as if uncomfortable with Mark's admission. "I treat my friends right."

"Thank you, Sam," Jodi said.

"Glad to see you lookin' out for him. I'd expect nothin' less from you." The chair creaked as Sam stood and stretched. "Oh, and just in case you need to keep that old hound dog in line, the code to the safe room is seven-two-six-one-nine. Maybe you could give Mark a turn being tied to the posts some day. Remind him who's in charge."

He walked to the door then paused, a smile slowly blossoming across his face. "But you might want to phone first."

With a wink, he left.

SHE FINALLY LOOKED UP AT MARK, worried that perhaps she'd overstepped the boundaries, but saw no sign of irritation or anger on his face. "I didn't mean to stick my nose where it didn't belong.

"Are you mad at me?"

Mark shook his head. "No. As Sam said, you were looking out for me." He laced his fingers with hers and tugged her back onto his lap. "Kind of nice to know you worry about me like that. Besides, as Hauberk's new vice president of Western Operations, it's a reasonable concern."

"Vice president?" A thrill shot through her at the

title until she remembered Mark's daily frustrations dealing with employees who were late or failed to show up at critical times. His anger when he caught several operatives smoking joints while on duty. And the mountains of paperwork that covered his desk. "Does that mean I have to sit behind a desk shuffling papers all day?"

Mark snorted. "As if that'll ever happen." When she tweaked a handful of chest hair, he sighed. "All right, there will be some paperwork involved. But you can hire an assistant if you need one. It also means you'll get to boss the guys around even more than you do now."

"I'm not bossy!"

He raised one eyebrow. "You just bullied a guy who's six foot six and weighs two eighty buck naked about the merger. That wasn't bossy?"

"That was…" she walked her fingers up his chest, "…a negotiation. On behalf of someone I love."

His hands slipped underneath the bottom of her shirt, cupped her breast with his palms, his thumbs brushing over the sensitive tips. "Hmm. I love hearing you say that."

She leaned into his touch, eyes closing. Talented fingers, she thought for what had to be the umpteenth time that night. "What? That I negotiated for you?"

"No, that you love me. You've never said that before."

The distinctive sound of a Harley revved outside. Jodi rushed to the window just in time to see Sam tugging on his helmet. "I knew I'd heard a motorcycle! But how'd he get in without me seeing it?"

She glanced back and saw Mark's lips clamp together, a telltale twitch at the side betraying his urge to smile.

"You! You came with him, didn't you?" She poked him in the chest and thought back to when he'd arrived, and what he'd done. "And then you deliberately distracted me from watching the monitors, didn't you? With that stupid vibrating egg!"

"Didn't take much effort," Mark said. He stood behind her, wrapping his arms about her waist as they watched Sam glance back at the house. He gave a salute toward them, then roared down the driveway.

CHAPTER ELEVEN

M ark turned her away from the window until she
faced him, then kissed her, his lips brushing
over hers in a featherlight touch. "*Te amo.*"

Jodi wrapped her arms about his neck, pulled him
closer until her breasts brushed his chest. "I love you
too."

Not knowing what was at the bottom of the chasm
he was about to leap into, he teetered on the edge. He
hated the strange feeling of fear curling in his bowels.
But there was no going back after tonight, there was no
way he could let her walk away with someone else.

She nestled her head in the crook of his shoulder,
rested her hand on his chest. Everything about her felt

so right.

"Babe? I, uh, have something to ask you." He swallowed hard. She'd said she loved him, but that didn't mean she wanted to marry him. *What if she said no?*

She pulled back to look at him, her eyes wide, almost fearful, held her body still. "What?"

He took a deep breath and leapt into his future. "Will you marry me?"

Jodi stiffened in his arms. "M-marry? Marry you?" The words seemed forced, as if they'd stuck in her throat.

Somewhere in the back of his mind, he'd wanted her to throw her arms about his neck and shout, "Yes, yes, yes! Of course, I'll marry you." Instead her hold on him loosened and blank shock filled her eyes. The bright light that he'd hoped would be his future turned out to be a heat-seeking missile racing toward him, its target his heart.

"I still want you to be vice president of Western Operations, whether you say no or not," he said quickly, wondering if she thought her answer might be tied to the promotion. "Sam and I discussed it already. I just hoped… I want to…" He stumbled on, unable to stop himself from babbling, knowing he was sounding like an idiot. "I love you and want to marry you."

She laughed, a half-hysterical sound he'd never heard from her before. Her head dropped onto his shoulder as her body rippled. Was she crying? Worse, she was laughing. No. Giggling!

"You…you…you want to m-m-marry me!" Her giggles reached an almost hysterical quality.

He'd bared his soul to her, asked her to marry him and she was giggling? His arms dropped as the missile hit its target and shredded his flesh, his soul. "I didn't think it was so funny."

"Oh, M-Mark," she choked out from behind the fingers she'd pressed over her mouth. "I'm sorry, I'm not laughing at you. I'm laughing at me."

Sure didn't feel that way.

"You see, tonight"—her giggles trailed off into a sigh—"tonight, when I was waiting for you in the van? I thought…I thought you were trying to brush me off, to dump me."

He felt his jaw drop. Dump her? After all he'd gone through to arrange this evening? Would he ever understand how women thought?

"Why?" he finally managed to splutter.

"Because you've been so distant lately." She held up

her hand when he started to protest. "It was like you were trying to avoid me. I-I thought maybe you'd gotten tired of me. I thought maybe you thought it was time to move on."

He scrubbed his hand through his hair. "I'm sorry—I've been busy arranging this evening with Sam, and hammering out the details of the merger. I never meant for you to feel like I was ignoring you."

"I know." She released a breath and her voice wavered. "No, I didn't know. I just kept remembering that agreement we made that either of us could walk away at any time, no questions asked."

He saw pain flicker through her eyes, realized she was remembering how she'd been treated by past lovers. Cursed himself for forgetting that beneath the tough exterior Jodi showed everyone else was a sensitive woman who needed reassurance that she could be herself without fear of rejection. He ran a finger along her jaw, marveling at how others didn't realize her tough shell was just an act. "I've just been distracted. I'm sorry. If I wasn't interested I would have told you straight out. I wouldn't have just walked away."

"I wasn't sure what you'd do," she said softly, not realizing how much it hurt him that she might think he could treat her so callously. "I figured you just might not know how to tell me. After all, we did agree that we wouldn't…you know…"

"Fall in love?" He captured her hand with his, pressed a kiss to her palm. "Jodi, I've never felt like this"—he moved her hand to his chest, flattened her palm over his heart—"about any other woman. Ever. I love you. And I want to marry you. Will you marry me, Jodi?"

She looked up at him, her bright blue eyes filled with tears. "Yes. Oh, Mark, of course I'll marry you."

He released the breath he'd been holding and enfolded her within the circle of his arms, held tight, realized he was shaking with the fear that had engulfed him that she might say no.

When he nuzzled his nose against the side of her neck, he frowned. He could still smell a trace of cigar—of Sam—in her hair. He silently cursed himself again for letting another man touch her, while thanking Sam for forcing the issue, for forcing him to acknowledge how much he loved the woman in his arms. His grip loosened from about her and he stepped back.

"Come with me." He held out his hand, waiting

until she put her palm into his.

Neither spoke while they walked down the hall. Mark led her up the stairs and to the bathroom they'd used earlier. When she'd brought him there earlier, she'd not wanted to let Sam between them yet. He wondered if she realized he felt the same way now.

He reached into the shower and turned on the water. When he was satisfied with the temperature he turned back to her. He grasped the hem of her T-shirt and pulled it over her head and discovered she wore no bra.

"So beautiful," he murmured. He cupped her breasts with his palms, bent his head and licked, savored.

Jodi arched, pressing her breasts deeper into his mouth. Her hands rested lightly on his shoulders, her thumbs caressing the sides of his neck. "Thank you for giving me a birthday I'll never forget." She chuckled. "It's not a story we can ever tell our children, but—"

"Children?" Mark breathed. His balls retracted in a painful clench. How had tonight gone from his planned night of debauchery to a discussion about marriage *and* kids? "You want kids?"

She jerked back, the smile dropping from her face.

"Don't you?"

"Yeah, yeah, I want kids," he quickly assured her while wondering if he did. His eyes dropped to her belly, imagined it swollen with his child. Imagined having a little boy he could play catch with. Maybe a little girl he could carry around on his shoulders. Yeah, he could do that. "Yeah, I want kids."

Maybe that would stop his younger brother José's ceaseless bragging about how he'd given their parents the first grandchild. Like the twerp had done it himself. His chest swelled as he pictured announcing to his brothers that he'd given their parents the first grandson—no, grandsons!—in the family. "Two. At least two."

Her smile returned. And with it his world returned to an even keel, although spinning faster than it had been before the evening had started.

"Let's start with one and see how we do from there, okay?" Jodi wrapped her arms about his neck and pulled him close. "But it may take some practice first."

"Practice. Yeah, practice is good." He pressed her against the tile wall. "For instance, I need lots of practice kissing you."

"Mmm." She turned her head, captured his lips with hers. What seemed like an hour later, they both came up for air. "What else do we need to practice?"

She caught her breath when she saw the dark embers deep in his eyes flare into wildfire. Why had she thought he didn't love her? It was there plain in his eyes. It was in his calloused fingers as he cupped her breasts, rolled her nipples between his fingers with a delicious pressure. In his voice, the trace of Spanish accent betraying the depth of his emotion as he spoke, "If we're going to have children, you're going to want to breastfeed them, right?"

She moaned as warm breath and warmer lips caressed her, teased her, tasted her. Cool air touched her bare skin when he pushed her jeans to the floor, his tongue never stopping its homage to her breasts. When he shifted, forcing her to arch her back, she dug her fingers into his shoulders and hung on. Hung on to the man she loved. Who loved her.

His clothes abandoned on the floor beside hers, Mark carried her into the shower, held her beneath the pulsing streams of water and began to wash her, his soapy hands lathering her shoulders, her breasts, her belly.

No inch of her escaped his attention. Where downstairs his lovemaking had been with a fierce desperation, now he took the time to caress her, to worship every part of her body. Every place he touched ignited until her blood boiled and her skin was ready to burst into flames.

WHEN HIS FINGERS DIPPED DEEP INTO HER HEAT, she arched into his touch. The rhythmic pounding of the shower on her skin was no match for the conflagration he fanned deep within her.

By the time he slid into her, Jodi was sure the smoke alarms would go off and the fire trucks would scream down the lane.

THE WATER HAD LONG SINCE GONE COLD, and they'd moved from the shower to the bed when Mark wrapped an arm around Jodi, tugging her back against him.

"I'm thinking we should look for a house in the Mid Cities, maybe Grapevine. One with lots of bedrooms."

His hand drifted to her belly. "And then I'm going to install a security system rivaling Fort Knox. After all, I can't have anyone else getting their hands on my private property."

Acknowledgments

To my husband who told me to "go for it" when I first mentioned that "maybe I should try to get published?"

To my eldest son who reminded me that I should put my money where my mouth was, especially since I'd told him that he should follow his dreams when looking for a career. And to my whole family, thank you for putting up with my endless discussions about writing and for answering my sometimes-obscure questions about how guys think. I love you all.

To Becky B. who has been there from the start. You poked and prodded and nagged me to submit to an agent or editor. I wouldn't be here without you, my friend. Thank you.

And to Tabatha, Margie, Fedora, Nikki, Lisa, Lori, Sharon, Sheri, Phuong, Kim and all the other members of my reader group over on Facebook who have become my cheering squad. And I mustn't forget Laura N who refers to herself now as Mrs. Sam Watson…I love you all!

About the Author

Leah Braemel is the only woman in a houseful of males that includes her college-sweetheart husband, two sons, a Shih Tzu named Seamus who behaves like a cat and Turtle the cat who thinks he's a dog. She loves escaping the ever-multiplying dust bunnies by opening up her laptop to write about sexy heroes and the women who challenge them.

Reviewers have awarded Leah's books numerous Top Pick and Recommended Reads designations as well as nominated them as Best Contemporary Romance, Best Erotic Romance and Best Ménage and More. Leah has also been nominated as Favorite Author and Best Erotic Romance Author.

Don't miss the next steamy novel in the
Hauberk Protection series.

Personal PROTECTION

By Leah Braemel

Available now from Somerlane Publishing

PERSONAL PROTECTION

The limo pulled into the underground parking lot and past his Jag. A sigh escaped Sam as they cruised past his Harley. The crisp October day would have been perfect to drive his Road King. Instead he was cooped up like a damned dog in the back of the limo that finally stopped near the elevator where Rosie was waiting.

Damn it, why had Chad insisted on Rosie Ramos as his lead CPO? If he'd wanted a woman to accompany him to any upcoming parties or meet 'n greets—the reason Chad had given him—why not McKee or Anderson? Neither of those women got his cock twitching like Rosie did.

The fantasy he'd had of getting her alone in his apartment hadn't included her wearing a gun and acting as his personal bodyguard. All right, maybe one had. But, damn it, if a bullet was going to be aimed in his direction, there was no way in hell he wanted the spitfire throwing herself in its path. He'd rather have her throw herself in his bed. Go down on her knees and unzip his fly… Damn it! Damn it! Damn it!

"All clear, Mr. Watson," Rosie said quietly.

"Of course it is." Sam ducked his head and clambered out of the limo, then stomped to the elevator. Goddamn it, she'd even acquired a key to the elevator, locking the door open so no one else could use it. He ignored that it was standard operating procedure and lashed out, "You think other people might not need the goddamned elevator?"

"Better than having the door open and somebody shoot you from inside. Besides there are other elevators still available."

Her voice was so damned reasonable. Placating. Like he was some baby to be soothed out of a tantrum.

Which is exactly how he was behaving but goddamn it, his people were supposed to be protecting others. Not him.

She turned the key and let the door close, pressing the button for the penthouse. The elevator began to rise, a quiet chime announcing each floor they passed. And with each ding, Sam became more and more aware of the delicate smell of apricot shampoo and woman filling the confined area. He closed his eyes, trying not to deliberately inhale great lungfuls of that amazing scent.

As long as she was around him, he'd not sleep.

Instead he'd be staring at the ceiling imagining what it would feel like to cup her breasts in his hands, to unzip her pants and nudge aside that blue thong. Imagine going down on her and tasting her honey. When she'd been in the gym doing those stretches, he'd obsessed about some of the positions she could get into while he fucked her. Then in his office while Chad had been briefing her, he'd pictured her stretched out over his desk, her legs hitched over his shoulders. And now she'd be in the next apartment, so damned available.

Damn it!

"Mr. Watson, do you have a problem with me guarding you?"

"Nope." He couldn't help that his answer sounded like a growl. He had one helluva a problem and at the moment it was punching against his zipper. He shifted his briefcase so she wouldn't see his hard-on.

"I mean, do you have a problem with a woman guarding you?"

Shit! She thought he didn't want her because she was a woman? Why not add sexual discrimination to the mix today? He exhaled and opened his eyes. "No, Ms. Ramos, I do not have a problem a female operative leading my team."

"Then do you have a problem with me personally?"

Was it a problem that he was imagining pinning her up against the wall and ramming into her until she screamed her release? How the hell did he explain that to her without getting slapped with a sexual harassment suit in addition to the discrimination one?

"If I didn't have complete confidence in your abilities, you wouldn't work for Hauberk, and Chad wouldn't have personally chosen you as team leader."

That must have been the answer she was looking for. She nodded, and her shoulders imperceptibly relaxed. "Thank you."

"I'm pis—ticked off at whoever is sending those damned photographs, and I fu—frickin' don't like having to accept that I had to ask my own people to protect me. Leaves me damned twitchy. So don't take my grouchiness personally, Ms. Ramos. It's not directed at you."

No, what was pointing directly at her was his goddamned dick.

DELIBERATE DECEPTIONS

A little lying and misdirection in the name of love is never wrong. Right?

Chad Miller once had the perfect life—a beautiful baby daughter, a loving wife, a promising career with the FBI. Within a year, he'd lost everything. Making Hauberk Protection a success salvaged his career, but he's never managed to get over the one fateful decision that spelled the end of his marriage.

For eight years, grief and guilt have haunted Lauren Miller's climb up the ranks of the Light Brigade, a secret international hostage rescue team. Now she's the target of a vengeful ex-Brigade operative who'll stop at nothing to take her down. Even if it means taking out everyone she cares about. Including Chad. Getting him to accept her as his bodyguard? It'll take some fast talking—and faster hands.

Trapped in a remote safe house with Lauren is the last place Chad ever wanted to be. He may finally have the chance to get some answers about why she ran, but with his hard-won defenses crumbling, he's having trouble remembering the questions. In the heat of their rekindled passion, Lauren struggles to keep her professional focus…and keep the secrets that could break his heart all over again.

Product Warnings

Angst dead-ahead! Lost love. Angst. Reunited lovers. Angst. Sex. More angst. And did I mention the angst? A box of tissues is definitely needed. But don't worry, there's still a Happy-Ever-After.

PERFECT PROPOSAL

Sometimes the best laid plans go every which way but the one you want…

Sam Watson wants to propose to the love of his life, Rosie Ramos, but all his previous attempts have been thwarted. Every. Single. Time. This time he's determined that nothing, and no one, will get in his way. No interruptions. No exceptions. Not from work, not by family busybodies, not even if the roses crucial to his plans are lost. Nothing will stop him.

If only someone had let Rosie in on his plans…

Warning: *Contains misguided intentions, a hunky hero with more than just a ring burning a hole in his pocket, and a spitfire girlfriend who counters her own proposal. The romance may be sweet but the sex is explicitly hot, hot, hot.*

HIDDEN HEAT

Be careful what you don't wish for. Fate might snatch it away.

When handling Hauberk's managers, efficiency is Sandy Hallquist's watchword. In her personal life? Excitement all the way, baby. That's why she escaped Minnesota—and her marriage-minded mother—for a job with one of the hottest bodyguard companies on the eastern seaboard. What more could she ask for than to be surrounded by all that alpha-male testosterone?

Invisibility is Troy's stock in trade, the only way he can manage Hauberk's international offices while answering the call of his other career: assassin. Nothing about him is real, not even his name.

In one moment of weakness, he allowed Sandy a glimpse behind his carefully crafted mask. The more he's around her, the sharper his yearning for stability. A home. Love. Pity those are the last things she's looking for. And revealing that she's the one true thing in his life could be the very words that drive her away.

At the first whisper of the "L" word, Sandy's first

instinct is to hit the brakes. By the time Sandy admits to herself that Troy is more than a passing fancy, though, his next mission could take the decision out of her hands.

Product Warnings

This book contains sexcapades in secret clubs, voyeurism, a touch of bondage and risqué office shenanigans.